THE THIRTEENTH CAT

MARY DOWNING HAHN

THE THIRTEENTH CAT

CLARION BOOKS

HOUGHTON MIFFLIN HARCOURT

BOSTON   NEW YORK

Clarion Books

3 Park Avenue

New York, New York 10016

Copyright © 2021 by Mary Downing Hahn

Clarion Books is an imprint of Houghton Mifflin
Harcourt Publishing Company.

hmhbooks.com

The text was set in Janson MT Std.

Cover art by Jeff Huang

Cover and interior design by Catherine Kung

The Library of Congress Cataloging-in-Publication Data is available.

ISBN: 978-0-358-39408-2

Manufactured in the United States of America

1 2021

4500829507

This book is dedicated to:

My niece Anne who gave me Nixi

My cat, Nixi, who inspired the story

My editor, Dinah, who helped me shape the story

THE THIRTEENTH CAT

1

LAST FALL, MY AUNT ALICE moved from a Boston suburb to Bexhill, a small town in Vermont. For the first time she had enough space for me to spend my summers with her instead of going to camp. Mom was delighted. She knew how much I hated camp, but even though I was almost thirteen, she didn't think I was old enough to spend my summers alone in Brooklyn while she worked. What could be better for me—and safer—than a summer in a small town?

When we pulled into her driveway, I thought my aunt's house was like something out of an old-fashioned kid's picture book, almost too pretty to be true, with flowers, blooming vines, and shade trees. There was even a front porch with a wooden swing at one end. All that was missing was a cat curled up on a mat by the front door. I hadn't been allowed to bring my cat, Suki, but I hoped to convince my aunt she needed a cat. I couldn't imagine living without one.

While we unloaded my luggage, I took a quick look at the neighbors on either side. On the right was a house similar to my aunt's—what people call a Victorian cottage, with dormers and fancy wood trim. Aunt Alice's house was yellow with blue trim, and the one beside it was blue with yellow trim. *Sweet,* I thought.

What really caught my attention, though, were the woods on the other side of my aunt's yard. The trees grew so close to a sagging wood fence that their branches hung over Aunt Alice's house. Some even brushed the roof.

Aunt Alice took one of my suitcases. "So, what do you think of my new home, Zoey?"

"It's wonderful!" I hugged her. "This is going to be the best summer ever!"

She hugged me back. "I've looked forward to it all year."

I followed her up the sidewalk. "Are those woods next door a park? Or a vacant lot?"

"Definitely not. Miss Dupree owns that land. No trespassers allowed."

I gazed at the woods longingly. "How would she know if someone trespassed?"

"What do you mean?"

"I don't see a house, so she must not live there."

"Oh, she lives there, all right. I've never seen the house, but it's hidden in there somewhere." Aunt Alice frowned. "She's very secretive and bad-tempered. She speaks to no one and no one speaks to her. I'm warning you, Zoey, don't put one foot on her property."

I followed my aunt inside, my thoughts on the mysterious Miss Dupree. I pictured a mean old lady wearing a baggy dress and dirty sneakers. But what was she really like? Maybe she wasn't as bad as my aunt thought.

Even though I'd been warned not to, I decided that exploring the woods was my first priority. Yes, I'd lounge in that porch swing, I'd read, I'd write in my journal, I'd enjoy a summer without camp counselors bossing me around, but all that could wait until I'd seen Miss Dupree and her house for myself.

Aunt Alice showed me my bedroom and left me to unpack while she fixed dinner. I spun around in a circle, arms outspread, grinning like an idiot. All this space! The room was at least twice the size of my room in Brooklyn. The windows were large and let in plenty of light, at least from the front—no fire escapes, no brick walls, no neighbors' windows, no rumble of traffic, no horns blowing, no sirens.

From the double windows, I saw my aunt's yard and a shady street. A woman walked a dog, a boy rode by on a bike, two little girls played hopscotch on the sidewalk. Somewhere a lawn mower droned.

Nice, but not as interesting as the view from the other window. From the side, I looked straight into the woods. The trees were so close that leaves brushed against the screen. Miss Dupree's property was deep and dark and endless, a forest in a fairy tale where nothing was what it seemed and danger lurked in the shadows. Witches, wicked fairies, enchantments good and bad—all the things I loved to read about.

What if I were a girl in such a forest, lost and afraid? Perhaps a witch lived there in a cottage. Perhaps she'd invite me in and cast a spell on me and keep me prisoner. Perhaps I'd be rescued. Perhaps I wouldn't be. Perhaps I'd find my own way home.

Maybe I'd write a story about that girl, but now I wanted to explore the woods in real life. I might come face-to-face with animals I'd never seen outside of a zoo — deer, raccoons, possums, foxes. Nothing big and dangerous, like a bear or a wolf. They probably lived in the mountains I'd seen in the distance.

***

When Aunt Alice and I sat down for dinner, I asked her if she'd ever met Miss Dupree.

"Once," Aunt Alice said. "It didn't go well."

"Why? What happened?"

"Not long after I moved here, I saw her walk past my house. I tried to introduce myself. You know, like people do. She looked me in the eye and said, 'No need for introductions. I keep to myself. That's why I have a fence. That's why I've posted No Trespassing signs.' I've never spoken to her again. Nor she to me."

I leaned across the table, eager to hear more about our strange neighbor. "What does she look like?"

"It's hard to say, Zoey. She's not really old but certainly not young. Not pretty but not ugly either." Aunt Alice sipped her iced tea. "She's average height, I'd say, and thin. Her hair's gray and she wears it in a knot at the nape of her neck."

She paused a moment before adding, "There's definitely something strange about her, maybe because she lives alone and hardly ever leaves her house. Maybe it's her cats — she has at least a dozen, all black, totally wild. The skinniest, ugliest cats I've ever seen. They roam the neighborhood, killing birds and terrifying pets — both cats and dogs. Children too."

Now I pictured Miss Dupree as a fierce old lady with her hair screwed tightly into a bun, still wearing a saggy dress and sneakers, but meaner than the grouchy old women in Brooklyn.

Aunt Alice surprised me by saying, "The few times I've seen her, she's been well dressed — beautifully tailored clothing, long, flowing scarves, that sort of thing. Very expensive, I'd say."

"Where does she go dressed up like that?"

"I have no idea, but sometimes she comes home in an old taxi. The driver usually follows her in. He leaves with an armload of boxes. He must deliver them for her."

"What's in the boxes?"

"No idea." She laid down her fork. "It's odd, now that I think about it, but I've never seen that cab anywhere else in town." She helped herself to another piece of chicken and passed me the platter.

While I ate, I made a plan to follow Miss Dupree the first time I saw her. I'd keep an eye out for the cab too.

Aunt Alice tapped my wrist to get my attention, the exact same thing Mom did. "You seem very curious about Miss Dupree. Believe me, she's a very unpleasant woman. Please stay away from her and her woods. When she says no trespassing, she means no trespassing."

I busied myself with my chicken. Aunt Alice was right. I was actually more than curious about Miss Dupree. She was a book I couldn't wait to read.

———

After dinner, Aunt Alice and I played a game of Scrabble. During the other times I'd visited, we'd settled into our own special routines. Scrabble after dinner. Pizza on Fridays. Eating out on Saturdays.

At the same moment when Aunt Alice won the game, Mom called. I told her about the woman next door and the woods, and she told me about her day at the office and the meeting she'd chaired. "Mr. Chaney was very pleased with me. I think I'm on track for either a bonus or a promotion — maybe both."

"That's great, Mom. Congratulations."

"Thanks, Zoey. I miss you, kiddo! The apartment is empty without you."

"I miss you too, Mom."

"If I know my sister, she'll keep you entertained. You won't be bored."

I asked her to put my cat on the phone. Even though I knew Suki didn't understand anything I said, I hoped she'd recognize my voice.

"I miss you so much, Suki. I wish you were here!"

Suki meowed once or twice but I couldn't be sure she knew it was me.

After Suki got off the phone, Mom asked to talk to her sister. I told her I loved her and handed the phone to Aunt Alice.

By then, I was so tired I could hardly keep my eyes open, but once I got into bed, I had trouble falling asleep. Maybe I wasn't used to absolute darkness. At home, a streetlight shone in my bedroom window. Headlights made tracks across my ceiling. Neighbors' lamps kept their windows lit long after I fell asleep.

Finally, I gave up and perched at the foot of my bed, staring out into the night. In the dark, the woods were even more mysterious. Fireflies winked on and off in the trees, like thousands of tiny Christmas lights. I could almost believe they were magic lanterns carried by invisible creatures like will-o'-the-wisps in fairy tales, as dangerous as they were beautiful.

I searched for a light from Miss Dupree's house, but the trees hid even the smallest glimmer. Maybe in the winter, when the trees were bare, you could see it. Unfortunately, I wouldn't be here then, unless Mom and I came for Christmas, but usually she had too much work to take off more than Christmas Day and sometimes Christmas Eve.

Though I didn't see anything, I heard a strange whirring noise. It came and went as if the night breeze carried it to me and then took it back. The sound must have been coming from Miss Dupree's house, but I couldn't figure out what made it. Maybe she had visitors. But that wasn't very likely. As far as I could tell, she was very unfriendly. Why would she invite anyone to her house?

After a while, I lost interest in the noise. It just went on and on, never changing, never giving a clue as to what made it. Shivering in the cold night air, I closed the window and slid under my covers. Surely, I would sleep now.

But I was as tense as ever. Right side, left side, on my back, and on my stomach, I flipped and flopped. I couldn't get comfortable no matter what I did.

If only Mom had let me bring my cat. Suki slept beside me every night. She purred in my ear and put me to sleep.

Without Suki's warmth to comfort me, I gave up and did an exercise my gym teacher taught us. Beginning with my feet, I relaxed my whole body piece by piece — toes, ankles, shin bones, knees, and so on, until I finally fell asleep.

2

I WOKE UP TO SUNSHINE and bird song. The woods were a dark shade of green shot through with yellow from the sun, still mysterious but nothing like last night.

Pulling a hoodie over my pajamas, I ran downstairs, hopping from step to step like a dancer in an old Fred Astaire movie. Aunt Alice was in the kitchen scrambling eggs. Sunlight shone in the window and the radio was tuned to classical music. From the back, she looked so much like my mother, I almost forgot Mom wasn't here.

"I was just about to wake you," Aunt Alice said. "I'm due at the library at eight thirty. I think I told you earlier, but I wanted to make sure you remembered." She poured herself a cup of coffee and set a plate of scrambled eggs, hash browns, and toast in front of me. "I ate already," she told me. "I was too hungry to wait for Miss Sleepyhead to get out of bed."

"Wow. This looks better than the breakfast Mom and I get at the diner." I picked up my fork and got to work on the eggs. "It tastes better too."

While I ate, I told Aunt Alice about the weird whirring sound. "Did you hear it?"

She shook her head. "My bedroom's on the other side of the house, but in all honesty, I sleep so soundly a tornado wouldn't wake me."

"Do you think it was cicadas?"

She shook her head again. "Too early in the summer to be cicadas."

"Maybe Miss Dupree had company," I suggested. "And the whirring noise was some sort of weird music."

"I can't imagine her having guests, Zoey."

"Well, what did I hear then?"

"Maybe you were dreaming. I've had dreams so real I woke up thinking they actually happened."

I ate a slice of toast spread thickly with Aunt Alice's homemade blackberry jam, the best I'd ever tasted. She could be right. I had vivid dreams too, but usually mine were about tsunamis or wars or maniacs climbing through my window to kill me. I was sure I'd been awake when I heard the whirring sounds.

Aunt Alice carried her cup to the sink. "What do you plan to do today?"

"Hang around the house, I guess. Maybe go for a walk."

She kissed me and picked up her purse. "See you around three. Thank goodness for summer hours."

After she left, I went to my room to get dressed and make my bed. As I was smoothing the spread, I heard a noise and looked out my open window.

Right below me, a big black cat slunk out of the woods. Several black cats, all long and skinny, followed the first one. Miss Dupree's cats, I supposed, just as mean and ugly as I'd imagined.

They looked up and saw me at the window. Their leader growled and laid back its ears, and the others lashed their tails and hissed. All of them, that is, except one—a small cat, not a kitten but full-grown, the runt of the litter maybe, as delicate and pretty as can be. She was totally out of place in that tribe of big mean cats.

Gazing up at me, she rose on her haunches like a meerkat, her eyes on me and me alone. If ever a cat needed a friend, she did.

The others skulked away through the weeds and brambles, but the small cat stayed where she was, looking right at me, just the way Suki did when she wanted something.

"Oh, you, you're so sweet," I called. "Come over here, and I'll feed you. You look so hungry."

The cat crept closer to the tall wooden fence dividing my aunt's yard from Miss Dupree's property. She hesitated, unsure of me, so I whispered again, "Kitty, kitty, kitty."

I held my breath as she put one paw under the fence, then another. Slowly she poked her head through the gap.

Just as she began to creep into my aunt's yard, the leader of the cats burst out of the weeds. The small cat whirled to face it.

With a savage smack, the big cat knocked her to the ground. The small cat rolled on her back and lay still, clearly giving up.

"Oh," I called to her. "Get up! Run! Don't let that bully hurt you!"

The big cat growled as if to say the small cat belonged to her. Giving her a vicious cuff, the bully chased her into the woods.

"You haven't won," I shouted after the cat. "Just wait and see. I'm going to rescue that cat and nothing you can do will stop me."

I ran outside to the fence. It was too tall to see over, but I found a loose board and pushed it aside. The cats were gone, as if they'd never been there. Somewhere in the woods a couple of crows cawed back and forth.

Later, after I'd eaten lunch, I sat in the porch swing and waited for Aunt Alice to come home. It was almost two. Only an hour to wait.

The summer had begun just as I'd imagined. I had a book and big glass of lemonade. I pushed my foot against the porch and the swing swayed gently.

After a few minutes, I heard a soft meow. The small cat sat on the porch railing and stared at me. Her eyes were pale green and as round and shiny as marbles.

"Well, hello, cat," I said. "Have you run away again?"

She twitched her tail and kept her eyes on me as if she had something important to say. Maybe she was hungry, maybe she wanted me to pet her, maybe she was just curious.

I patted my lap. "Come here, cat, and tell me everything."

Instead of accepting my invitation, she stayed where she was and washed her face, never looking away from me.

"Are you hungry?"

Still watching me, she continued grooming herself. Everything about her was neat and dainty.

"Do you like tuna?" I asked her.

Her ears flicked and she meowed so softly I barely heard her. I stood up, expecting her to run but glad she stayed where she was.

"Wait right there." I went inside, opened a can of tuna, and put a dab on a saucer. Moving slowly so as not to scare her, I put the food on the porch floor. Without making a sound, she jumped down from the railing and sniffed the tuna. In less than a minute, she was licking the empty plate.

I gave her another helping and sat beside her on the porch floor. Cautiously I reached out and stroked her. She was so thin I felt her spine and her ribs. Instead of running, she purred.

"Do you want to stay here with me?" I whispered.

Her purr became a rumble and she rubbed her head against my leg. She might as well have said yes.

"You'll be safe here. I won't let those horrible cats come near you." I stroked the soft place under her chin. "How did you ever end up with them?"

Suddenly her back arched and she whirled around. The leader of the cats jumped onto the railing. The small cat leapt from my lap and darted into the bushes. The mean one ran after her.

The small cat raced ahead as if her life depended on getting away. The big one drove her toward the fence and chased her under it. Close behind, I shoved the loose board aside and ran after them.

The cats bounded down a narrow, twisting path that led into the woods. Ignoring the No Trespassing signs, I followed. Nothing would stop me from rescuing that cat, not even Miss Dupree herself.

With every step I took, the woods grew denser and darker. The humid air hummed with gnats and mosquitoes. My T-shirt clung to my back like a wet rag. Sweat poured down my face and dripped from my chin. I would have paid twenty dollars for a bottle of water.

Gradually the trees thinned out and I came to a clearing. A house loomed up in front of me. Boards covered the first-floor windows, and the windows on the second floor were barred. It looked more like a prison than someone's home. The witch in my fairy tale could have kept the lost girl here, locked in a room with bars on the window.

I crouched at the edge of the woods and watched the house. It looked deserted, but Miss Dupree must have been inside. Surely, she'd heard me crashing through the woods, calling the cat.

But the house was silent. Miss Dupree didn't come out to chase me away. Like a mouse, I waited for the cat to pounce.

Minutes passed with no sign of her. Hoping to be less visible, I hunched over and crept along a path to the back of the house. Crooked stairs led to a small porch. A No Trespassing sign was nailed to the door, its letters scrawled in red paint.

Keeping my head down, I tiptoed slowly around the corner, sure that Miss Dupree was watching every step I took, hearing every sound I made. The fierce summer heat made me itch all over.

Where were the cats? I looked back to make sure they weren't sneaking up on me, but nothing moved in the weeds. It was like everything held its breath and waited to see what happened next.

Finally, I heard a faint meow. I got down on my hands and knees and crawled through the weeds and bushes, pushing past brambles with sharp thorns, searching under every branch for the little cat.

At last, I found her crouched by the house, her back pressed against the wall. I stretched my hand toward her. "Kitty, kitty," I whispered.

She looked at me but didn't move. When I crawled closer, I saw why. Almost hidden by tangled vines and bushes, the other cats huddled in a semicircle around the small cat. Their heads swung toward me and they growled, as if daring me to come nearer.

"Shoo," I whispered. "Go away. Scat!"

They lashed their tails, but otherwise they didn't move. The little black cat didn't move either. She watched the others as if she was just as scared of them as I was.

"I'm not afraid of you," I lied to the cats. With a quick move, I scooped up the small cat and got to my feet.

"We're leaving now," I told the others. "Okay?"

It wasn't okay. They crept toward me slowly, their bellies pressed to the ground as though they were stalking a mouse. Their eyes gleamed, their tails whipped back and forth.

Holding the small cat, I backed away. "Scat!" I whispered. "Scat!" As if to help, the cat in my arms hissed at them.

They continued to move toward me, and I continued to edge away, afraid to turn my back on them. I'd never been afraid of cats or even dogs, but these weren't like any cats I'd ever met. There were so many of them, and they all looked like they wanted to kill me.

I tripped on something and fell flat on my back with the cat still clasped in my arms.

The others snarled and ran forward, but before they reached me, a low voice called, "That's enough, my dears, leave them to me."

Without letting go of the small cat, I staggered to my feet. Half-hidden in shadows, a thin woman strode down the porch steps. Her face was pale and sharp featured, her mouth thin lipped, her eyes darkened with makeup. She wore a dark red dress, and a black-and-white scarf fluttered around her neck. A long-haired white cat followed her.

It was Miss Dupree herself, just as my aunt had described her but much scarier.

"What do you think you're doing?" Her voice was slightly accented and harsh. "Put that cat down at once! She belongs to me."

The small cat's sharp claws bit through my shirt and into my skin. She laid her ears back and hissed as if daring Miss Dupree to take her from me.

"She was in my yard," I said, "and one of your cats chased her into the woods. I rescued her and I'm taking her home with me." I was scared, but I was not giving this poor shivering cat to that woman.

"You have no right to be on my property or to help yourself to one of my cats." She directed my attention to the sign on her door. "Is it presumptuous to assume you know how to read?"

"I'm not leaving without this cat." I'd never spoken to an adult so rudely, but I was more angry than scared now.

"Well, Zoey, perhaps I should tell your aunt how defiant you've been. She'll be shocked to hear you tried to steal my cat."

I stared at her. "How do you know my name?"

"Oh, I know all about you, Zoey." She came toward me, stopping when she was less than a foot away. This close, her eyes were a strange shade of pale green flecked with yellow. In the sunlight, her pupils were tiny black dots.

I stepped back, frightened of her eyes and the way they peered into mine, as if she could read every thought I'd ever had. I held the hissing cat tightly, but my legs trembled. It seemed the cat was braver than I was.

As I stepped backward, Miss Dupree stepped forward, like we were doing a strange dance. "Thirteen is mine. She belongs here with her sisters. I have no patience with bratty children who trespass on my property and torment my cats."

She made a sudden move and yanked the cat she called

Thirteen from my arms. The cat struggled, scratched, and bit, but she couldn't break the woman's grip on her.

Shaking the angry cat, Miss Dupree said, "Be still, Thirteen! Do not fight me. You are mine, not hers."

"Give her back!" I cried. "Give her back!" I reached for the cat, but the others wove themselves into a tight circle around me. One bit my ankle. Another scratched my leg, drawing blood.

"Please," I begged. "You have so many cats. Why can't you let me have her?"

The cats snarled louder. They pressed against me so tightly I couldn't move. One bit my ankle again, harder this time, and I cried out in pain.

"Let her go, my dear girls." Miss Dupree made a strange fluttering gesture with her hand, and the cats immediately broke their circle and ran to her side.

She turned to me. "Leave my property now and never come here again." She stepped closer as if she was about to tell me a secret. "Thirteen is *mine,* Zoey. Nothing you do can change that."

Miss Dupree carried the struggling cat into her house. The white cat followed closely at her heels. The black ones flowed behind them. The door shut with a bang that shook the flimsy porch.

3

SOBBING WITH ANGER AND FEAR, I ran back through the woods. Briars scratched my legs. Mosquitos and gnats bit me. I fell and cut my knee on a sharp stone.

The woods seemed endless. Tree roots spread everywhere, humping out of the ground, tripping me.

Where was the fence? Where was Aunt Alice's house? All I saw were trees, trees, trees, all around me, blocking my way, blocking my view.

I must have run in circles, passing the same trees again and again. Breathing hard, I stood still for a moment. The woods spun in a green blur. My head felt like it was spinning with them. I staggered and grabbed hold of a tree to keep from falling.

I breathed deeply and closed my eyes for a moment. When I opened them, I realized the fence was only a few feet away, almost hidden in the underbrush. Beyond it was the safety of Aunt Alice's house.

I wiggled through the gap and collapsed on the grass. I was safe, but my heart still pounded. I felt like laughing hysterically, but I cried instead.

When my heart slowed to normal, I stood up slowly, still feeling kind of shaky. Beyond the fence, the woods were still and peaceful. A thrush sang, and the afternoon sun slanted down through the trees. It must have been after three, which meant my aunt was home.

I ran across the yard and into the kitchen. And there she was, sitting at the table reading the *New Yorker*, a glass of iced tea beside her. She looked up, startled, as I threw myself into her arms.

"Zoey," she gasped, "what's wrong? You're covered with scratches and bug bites. Are you all right?"

"Oh, Aunt Alice," I sobbed. "There was this sweet little cat, she came from next door and I fed her, and then a big ugly, horrible cat chased her into the woods, and I ran after her. And, and—"

I held on tighter. "Miss Dupree came outside and yelled at me, and she took the little cat away. I was so scared. She was really mad, and her eyes . . . they were . . . oh, I can't tell you how they were, you'd have to see them. It's like she looked in my brain and read my thoughts."

"Oh, Zoey, Zoey." Aunt Alice hugged me and stroked my back. "I told you not to go near her or her property."

"Don't be mad, please don't be mad. I just wanted to save the little cat."

My aunt hugged me again. "It's all right. I'm not mad. I know how much you love cats." She handed me her iced tea. "Here, drink this. You need it more than I do."

I thanked her and drank the tea in big hiccupping gulps. "If

I see that little cat again, I'll bring her inside where she'll be safe. Miss Dupree won't dare to come inside your house!"

Aunt Alice stroked my hair. "Oh, Zoey, you can't take her cat just because you don't like the way she treats it."

"But if you saw the cat, Aunt Alice, you'd understand. She's so skinny you can feel her bones. And the other cats gang up on her. I've seen them."

"Let's talk about the cat later." She patted my head like I was a scared child in need of comforting. "Right now, I want you to take a deep breath and calm down. I've never seen you so upset."

With her arm around me, she led me to the bathroom and went to work on my scratches with soap and water and disinfectant.

"Did you ever tell Miss Dupree about me?" I asked her.

"Of course not. I never talk to her. Why?"

"She knew my name."

Aunt Alice thought about that and shook her head. "She must have heard me call you."

"Maybe she spies on us."

"Why would she be interested in what we say or do?"

I watched her tape a bandage neatly on my knee. "Maybe because she's crazy."

"Oh, Zoey, please don't throw that word around. Miss Dupree is just a strange old woman. Think how unhappy she must be, living alone with those dreadful cats to keep her company. No wonder she wants the one you tried to rescue. She must be the only nice cat in the bunch."

Aunt Alice put the first-aid supplies away. "Promise to stay away from her. And her cats."

Later, when I'd calmed down, Aunt Alice and I sat on the front porch, side by side in the swing, and rocked gently back and forth. The evening air was cool and the first stars had begun to appear.

"How would you like to meet me at the library tomorrow and have lunch somewhere special?" Aunt Alice asked.

I snuggled closer to her. "I'd love to."

"I might even have a surprise for you," she murmured.

"What?"

She laughed. "It won't be a surprise if I tell you."

"Is it animal, vegetable, or mineral?"

"My lips are sealed." She smoothed my hair. "You'll just have to wait until tomorrow."

The next day, when I left to meet Aunt Alice at the library, I saw three of Miss Dupree's ugliest cats sitting on the fence as if they were waiting for me. They watched me walk past, but they didn't move. The cat called Thirteen was nowhere to be seen.

Aunt Alice had told me to turn right on Benton Street, which took me past Miss Dupree's yard. The woods pressed up against her fence. Tree roots burrowed under the sidewalk and pushed its cement slabs up in uneven humps. The branches hung so low, I had to duck under them. A No Trespassing sign hung from a padlocked gate, and a narrow dirt path led through waist-high weeds into the woods. The only clue that a house was there was dozens of local newspapers wrapped tightly in plastic bags, littering the sidewalk.

I pictured Miss Dupree watching me the way her cats did, maybe plotting to get even with me for trying to steal poor Thirteen. I'd seen plenty of strange old women in Brooklyn, but they hadn't scared me the way Miss Dupree did. Maybe it was her eyes, but . . . no, it was more than that. The old women who sat beside me on the subway and told me about weird conspiracies and alien invasions made me uncomfortable, but I never thought they'd hurt me.

That was the difference between them and Miss Dupree: she could hurt me.

I ran past her yard and didn't slow down until I was at least a block away. Except for Miss Dupree's place, it seemed like a nice neighborhood. Most of the houses were old-fashioned like my aunt's, Victorian style, I thought. Some were bigger, some smaller, some newer, some older. Their lawns were mowed, their flower beds weeded, their bushes trimmed. Normal-size trees shaded the sidewalk. Birds sang. A woman walking her dog smiled and said hello.

I walked a few more blocks and came to the library, a small stone building with steps leading to glass doors. Very solid. Very old. Inside I followed an arrow to the children's department and asked a girl shelving books where my aunt was.

"Miss Fitzhugh's in the meeting room doing origami with

the summer reading club." The girl looked at me and grinned. "Wait, you must be Zoey! Your aunt said you were meeting her for lunch and she invited me to come too. I'm Lila. I live right across the street from your aunt—and you!"

She stopped talking for a second and looked around. "If Mrs. Walters catches me talking instead of shelving, I'll be chopped liver. She's such an old crab."

Pushing her book cart, Lila led me to a back corner where the shelves hid us from the librarian's desk. "This is my secret place to read. I shelve so many good books, sometimes I just have to stop and read for a while. Your aunt caught me once. She said reading was more important than shelving, but not to let Miss Walters see me because *she* thinks shelving is more important."

"This is a good place to hide from her," I said. "You even have a window so you can see what's going on in the park."

"As if anything ever is." Lila flicked a strand of long dark hair out of her face. "This town is soooo boring."

"Not if you live next door to Miss Dupree and her cats."

Lila's eyes widened. "She's the most hateful person in the whole town. Seriously. Have you met her?"

"Not on purpose. This sweet little cat came into my yard. I was making friends with her when one of the other cats chased her back into Miss Dupree's yard. I ran after her."

Lila grabbed my arm. "Wait—you went into her yard?" She stared at me in awe. "Nobody has ever done that, not even on a Halloween dare."

"I wasn't even thinking about Miss Dupree. All I wanted to do was grab that cat and take her home with me. But all of a sudden, there she was, yelling at me."

"I'd have fainted then and there," Lila said. "Dead on the ground. Cat food for sure."

"You can't imagine how terrified I was. She has the scariest eyes. It's like she can read your mind or something."

"You are totally brave, Zoey. As much as I loved my dog, I didn't have the nerve to follow him onto her property . . . even though I might have saved his life, which I didn't know at the time."

"What did she do to your dog?"

"Rusty chased one of her cats into her woods, and she saw him. I heard her screaming at him. And then he came running out of the woods, wild-eyed because he was so scared. That night he died a horrible death, even though he was young and healthy and the vet couldn't find any reason for his heart to stop. I *know* she poisoned him. My parents aren't totally sure because whatever she did left no trace, but they definitely suspect her."

"That's terrible, Lila. She's just the kind of person who'd poison a dog."

A woman poked her nose around the shelves. "Lila Perkins, I can hear your voice from the desk. You get busy shelving those books. Socialize on your time, not the library's time."

"Oh, sorry, Mrs. Walters." Lila shoved *Grimms' Fairy Tales* into an empty space on the shelf. "Do you know who this girl is?"

The librarian glanced at me and shook her head.

"She's Miss Fitzhugh's niece, Zoey. I just met her. We're all going to lunch together."

Mrs. Walters gave me a very small smile, the kind you make if your tooth hurts. "Oh, yes, of course, Zoey. Your aunt told me you're spending the summer with her. Lovely to meet you." She turned to walk away, but before she left, she looked at Lila. "Be sure the cart is empty before you leave for lunch."

Lila made a face at Mrs. Walters's back.

"I'd better go," I told her. "I'm getting you in trouble."

"Your aunt's in the meeting room downstairs," she said. "The program will be over soon, which is good because I'm starving."

When I found the meeting room, I saw nine or ten kids coming out. Each one carried a handmade origami crane and a library copy of *Sadako and the Thousand Paper Cranes,* one of my favorite books in third grade, even though I cried every time I read it.

"Guess who I just met," I said to Aunt Alice. "Lila Perkins!"

She laughed. "Lila was supposed to be the surprise at lunch. I think you two will hit it off. She's a darling."

"I liked her right away. But I felt sorry for her when Mrs. Walters caught us talking in the back of the room. She got all cranky with poor Lila."

"Poor Lila indeed." Aunt Alice smiled. "She's always in trouble, either for talking or reading when she should be shelving. Nobody, including Edna Walters, can stay angry with her for long. She's a good worker when she puts her mind to it."

"Did you know Miss Dupree poisoned Lila's dog?"

Aunt Alice sighed. "The whole family is convinced the dog was poisoned, but nobody, not even the vet, can prove it."

"What do *you* think?"

Aunt Alice shrugged. "I really don't know, but if Rusty injured the cat, she just might—"

At that moment, Lila joined us, and my aunt never finished the sentence.

———

Aunt Alice took Lila and me to Nixi's Café, a friendly place with a shady deck. We sat outside at a table with a view of the park. Aunt Alice ordered a giant salad, and Lila and I had cheeseburgers and french fries.

While we ate, I learned that Lila was twelve, like me, and starting eighth grade in the fall, also like me. We were both big fans of anime. Her favorite movie was *Spirited Away* and so was mine. We also loved fantasy and fairy tales and mysteries. I liked Sherlock Holmes but she liked Agatha Christie. Neither one of us liked *Stranger Things*. We both watched old TV shows like *Bewitched*. We were obviously meant to be friends, which made Aunt Alice happy.

4

AFTER LUNCH, AUNT ALICE went back to the library, but Lila was done for the day.

"Let's walk home through the park," she said. "It's cooler because of all the trees."

Near the lake, we found a grassy place in the shade and lay down to rest. Both of us had eaten way too many french fries and were about to burst. The sun filtered through the leaves and dappled us with shadows. Our stomachs began feeling better, but we stayed where we were and let the breeze tickle our noses.

Lila told me about this boy she liked named Justin. "He doesn't know I'm alive, but maybe he'll be in some of my classes this fall and, well, who knows what might happen." She propped herself up on one elbow. "Do you have a boyfriend?"

"No way. I go to an all-girls school in the city. But there's this red-haired boy I see on the subway sometimes. Once I think he smiled at me, and my heart kind of flipped or something. I kind of like him, but I don't even know his name."

While we talked, the ants discovered our legs. We brushed them off but they came back. I sat up and looked around for a better place to talk. On top of a hill near us was a row of benches. All of them were empty—except one.

I nudged Lila. "You won't believe this, but Miss Dupree is sitting on a bench right there." I pointed uphill behind her back.

Lila jumped up so fast she almost tripped over her own feet. "What's *she* doing here?"

"I don't know, but it sounds like she's talking to someone."

"Let's spy on her," Lila said.

"What if she sees us?"

"We'll be so quiet she won't hear us. She's probably half-deaf anyway."

The two of us sneaked up the hill, trying hard not to step on a twig or rustle the leaves. When we were as close as we dared to get, we crouched in the bushes behind her. No one was with her, but she was definitely talking to somebody.

I thought she was probably on the phone, but Lila could see her hands and whispered no, she must be talking to herself. She twirled her index finger and made a face.

Miss Dupree had what Mom called a carrying voice. Though she spoke low, we heard every word. "She's definitely living up to my impression of her. Nosy. Rude. Irritating. Extremely unlikeable." She paused as if waiting for an answer.

Although no one else spoke, she went on. "Most likely we'll need to do something about her."

Lila and I looked at each other. Who was she talking about? Lila mouthed, "The little cat?"

That made sense. *She's mad because the cat ran away. But what does do something about her* mean? I didn't like the sound of it.

Miss Dupree sighed. "Why can't they all be like you, dear one? Never a moment's trouble. Always sweet and biddable."

To my amazement, a white cat rose into sight and nuzzled Miss Dupree's ear.

Maybe I gasped in surprise, maybe Lila made a noise in the shrubbery, but Miss Dupree whirled around and saw us. "You nasty little sneaks, how dare you spy on me!"

The white cat laid back its ears and hissed.

Lila and I backed away. In too much of a hurry to watch where I was going, I tripped and tumbled down the hill. Lila slid after me. We landed in a heap at the bottom, muddy, our elbows and knees scraped and bruised.

With the white cat at her side, Miss Dupree glared down at us, eyes hidden behind dark sunglasses. Her black flowered dress swirled in a breeze, and her red scarf fluttered. A few stray hairs escaped her bun and blew in her face.

"Too bad you didn't break your necks," she said. "Maybe next time you won't be so fortunate." Without another look at us, she walked away. The cat ran beside her, her tail waving like a plume.

We scrambled to our feet and headed for the path, expecting to see Miss Dupree somewhere ahead of us, but nobody was there.

"Where did she go?" Lila asked.

I shook my head, as puzzled as she was. "Maybe she knows a shortcut or something."

Lila shook her head. "No way. We were right behind her." She paused a moment and stared at me. "Don't laugh, Zoey, but what if she made us fall down that hill?"

"How could she do that?"

"She killed Rusty, didn't she?"

"Nobody ever proved it."

"So what? A witch casts spells that leave no evidence." Lila sounded scared.

"Come on, Lila. You can't seriously think she's a witch." Even though the sun shone and I was hot, I shivered. For years, I'd wondered about witchcraft and magic and spells, but no one else, especially Mom, ever admitted things like that could possibly exist.

"I *am* serious!" Lila's face turned red. "Guess where the library shelves books on witchcraft? In nonfiction. What does that tell you?"

"Fairy tales and poetry and mythology are all in nonfiction," I told her.

"There's a reason for that. Your aunt explained it to me once, but I forget now."

"Okay, okay," I said. "If she's a witch, why doesn't she wear long black dresses and pointy hats?"

"That is such a cliché." Lila shook her head. "Modern witches look like everyone else."

"Next you'll tell me that woman over there is a witch." I pointed at a plump lady sitting on a bench, talking on a phone.

"That's just it, Zoey. She *could* be a witch. How do you know she's not?"

"Do you also believe in Bigfoot and the Loch Ness monster?"

Lila shrugged. "They're in nonfiction too."

I took a long look at Lila. She seemed like a normal person. Long brown hair, pretty face, wearing the kind of clothes everybody wore. Nothing strange or weird about her. "Are you telling me you really, truly think Miss Dupree killed your dog with a spell?"

"With my whole heart," Lila said. "It explains why the vet couldn't tell us why Rusty died."

"But, Lila—"

She cut me off. "Let me tell you something. Your aunt herself told me the two books most often stolen from libraries are Bibles and witchcraft books."

"Really? Aunt Alice said that?"

"Yep, she sure did. She was talking about books that tell you how to become a witch and how to cast spells. Serious books for serious witches. Not kid stuff."

"What does that prove?"

"If nothing else, it proves there's a lot of would-be witches out there stealing how-to books."

I held my hands up as if to say stop. "No more witches—my brain is melting."

We walked on, trying to stay in the shade. Even though I didn't want to talk about witches, I couldn't stop thinking about them. What if Lila was right? Suppose witches went about their business so quietly that nobody ever noticed them? Even someone as strange as Miss Dupree blended into the neighborhood as a cranky, peculiar old woman. I was pretty sure no one except Lila thought Miss Dupree was a witch.

Maybe her kind lived everywhere. There was one in our apartment building. Miss Stabler on the first floor had so many cats that her part of the hall always smelled like cat pee. She complained about the noisy people who lived in the apartment above hers and yelled at the maintenance man and scared kids like me if she caught us playing on the front stoop. I'd never thought of her as a witch, but what if she was?

Lila interrupted my thoughts. "To get back to your favorite crazy old lady who is not a witch, you can't deny Miss Dupree was talking to that white cat like it understood every word she said."

"You should hear me talking to my cat."

"But I bet you don't wait for it to answer."

I wasn't about to tell Lila that sometimes I did catch myself waiting for Suki to say something. She always seemed to understand every word. In a fake spooky voice, I said, "Maybe the white cat is her familiar."

Although I hadn't been serious, Lila agreed at once. "That totally explains it, Zoey. Witches always have familiars. Usually they're cats."

By then we were home. Lila pointed at the cats sitting on

the fence. "Remember the flying monkeys in *The Wizard of Oz*? Those cats are Miss Dupree's minions for sure. She told them to sit there and watch you. It's so obvious."

"If you'd ever had a cat of your own, you'd know they never do anything you tell them."

"These aren't ordinary cats," Lila said. "They belong to a witch."

"Oh, Lila, I'm already scared of those cats and Miss Dupree. Do you have to make it worse with all this witch stuff?"

"Confess, Zoey, you already believe it but you just won't admit it." Lila laughed. "Tomorrow's another library day for me, but I'll see you the day after. Maybe we can go to the swimming pool. No witches there!"

"That's a great idea!" I waved goodbye and crossed the street.

The cats watched me silently from the fence. I counted nine this time, but Thirteen was not with them.

"Go away, you ugly things," I muttered. "Stop watching me!"

The leader hissed. The others twitched their skinny tails and glared.

Once I'd shut the front door behind me, I peeked out the window. The cats were still on the fence. They turned to look at the window as if they knew I was there.

I yanked down the shade and retreated to the kitchen. Something about those cats bothered me. It wasn't natural to watch people the way they watched me.

But what if Lila was right about them? What if they were there to keep me away from Thirteen? It made sense in a weird way.

I shook my head. *Don't be silly, Zoey. Before you know it, you'll believe Miss Dupree really is a witch and those cats obey her orders.*

And that is ridiculous.

———

When Aunt Alice came home, I told her about seeing Miss Dupree in the park. "She was talking to her big white cat. When she saw us, she got mad. Lila says she made us fall down a hill. Lila thinks she's a witch, a real one."

"Oh, for goodness' sake." Aunt Alice fixed herself a cup of coffee and handed me a soda. "I'm sure you don't believe that."

"I don't know. When I was little, I was scared of the witch under my bed. Mom told me the only things under there were dust balls and a stray sock or two. Maybe a lost library book. Maybe some candy wrappers. But no witches. They were in stories, not real life."

"And you believed her, right?"

"Mom's very smart and well informed. She reads the *Wall Street Journal* and the *New York Times*. If she doesn't believe in magic or astrology or ESP or ghosts, maybe I shouldn't . . . but she's never met Miss Dupree."

"Your mother is very practical. If she met Miss Dupree, she'd probably report her to county health services as a person in need of help."

I laughed because that was exactly what Mom would do. "But what about you, Aunt Alice? Do you agree with Lila?"

She smiled. "Lila is very imaginative—and so are you."

"But do you think Miss Dupree is a witch?" I was really losing patience. "Just give me a straight yes or no. Is she a witch or not?"

She shook her head. "As much as I love fairy tales and folk tales, I find it nearly impossible to believe Miss Dupree's a witch or even that witches exist outside of stories. Perhaps you and Lila need to rein in your imaginations before they run away with you."

I wasn't sure whether I was relieved or disappointed by what Aunt Alice said. On the plus side, Miss Dupree could yell and carry on as much as she wished, but she couldn't put a spell on me. On the other hand, I hated being told to rein in my imagination. It was just the sort of thing Mom would say.

———

The next day I asked Aunt Alice if I could be a page at the library like Lila.

"Before you arrived, I asked if we needed another page, but it seems we have all the kids we can use. You're welcome to hang out and read, as long as you and Lila don't talk too much."

"Maybe I'll come over this afternoon," I told her. "Lila and I could walk home together."

"That's a splendid idea." She gave me a kiss and whispered, "No encounters with Miss Dupree!"

I watched her leave. Since Lila was scheduled to shelve books this morning, I was on my own — just me and the cats on the fence and Miss Dupree.

5

I POKED AROUND THE HOUSE for a few hours, entertaining myself by texting my friends who were dying of boredom at summer camp. I told them about Lila and the cranky woman next door with a hundred ugly black cats but didn't say anything about Lila's claim that Miss Dupree was a witch. They might think Lila was weird and maybe me too.

After that, I played solitaire on my iPad. Bored with losing to myself, I switched to Netflix and watched an episode of *Bewitched*. If I had to live next door to a witch, why couldn't she be nice and funny like Samantha?

Tossing my iPad aside, I found a bag of Oreos and ate most of them. I was even more bored than my friends at camp.

A few hours later, I made a peanut butter sandwich and ate it for lunch, along with the rest of the Oreos. Boredom made me hungry. If I didn't find something to do, my clothes would be too small by the end of the summer.

The day was cloudy, with storms predicted, but at least it was cooler than yesterday. If the sun had been out, I would have taken a walk in the park and gone to the library to meet Lila and Aunt Alice, but I didn't want to get soaked in the rain.

I looked out the living room window to see what the cats were doing. Twelve of them this time. The only ones missing were Thirteen and the white cat. They sat in a row on the fence, watching and waiting for me to come outside and start some trouble. No surprise there.

Why not make their day? Grabbing my iPad, I went outside and sat in the swing.

When the cats heard the door close behind me, they twitched their tails. The leader gave me a narrow-eyed look. The others stretched and yawned and scratched their fleas, but somehow no matter what they did, they never took their eyes off me.

I opened my iPad and began reading *The Once and Future King,* one of my absolute favorite books. I'd read it so often I knew every twist and turn of the plot. No surprises, just the pleasure of being in Camelot with Wart and Merlyn and all the others, both good and bad but never boring.

The cats' eyes seemed to crawl all over me, always watching, never blinking, never moving. I kept looking at them to make sure they weren't creeping across the grass to attack me.

I'd been sitting in the swing for only a few minutes when I noticed the cats' attention had shifted from me to something in in the weeds by the fence.

What did they see? As soon as I left the porch to find out, the cats were on their feet, hissing and growling. The leader arched her back like a Halloween cat and spat.

"I live here," I told them. "Get used to it."

I took a step closer, and the others arched their backs and puffed their tails, their ears flat against their heads. Their eyes gleamed.

By now, the clouds were moving in, darker and bigger than before. A breeze turned the leaves so their white sides showed—a sure sign of rain according to Aunt Alice.

Suddenly, Thirteen ran out of the weeds and came straight toward me. The other cats deserted their posts on the fence and went after her like a black wave spreading across the grass.

The little cat changed direction, crossed the street, and darted into Lila's yard.

Instead of chasing her, the cats ran back under the fence and disappeared into Miss Dupree's yard, yowling as if they were telling her that Thirteen was on the run again.

I followed the cat into Lila's yard. Frantic to rescue her, I searched the bushes and called to her softly. At last, in the shadows under the back porch, I saw her eyes shining in the dark. Slowly she crept toward me, her belly to the ground. Her big ears twitched this way and that as if she were listening for the other cats.

"Good girl, good girl." I held out my hand. Her nose moved slowly across my palm as if she were reading a book. I wanted to grab her and run for home, but I waited for her to come closer.

Finally, she sniffed my face. Her whiskers tickled my nose. Taking care to move slowly, I picked her up. She was so light, poor little thing, just fur and bones, as delicate as a kitten.

"Pretty girl, pretty girl," I whispered. "You're so brave."

With Thirteen in my arms, I came around Lila's house only to see Miss Dupree on the sidewalk in front of my house, surrounded by her cats. Thunder muttered and the wind blew harder. A car drove by with its headlights on, ready for rain.

For a moment, Miss Dupree and I faced each other, me on one side of the street, her on the other. A wave of hatred crossed the space between us and smashed against me. Overhead, thunder boomed, and I took a few steps back.

"Give me the cat, Zoey," Miss Dupree said. "We've been through this before."

"No!" I held Thirteen tighter. "I'll never let you have her!"

Before I knew what was happening, Miss Dupree was right in front of me, reaching for the terrified cat. Just as her long fingernails sank into Thirteen's neck, I ducked away from her and ran like I'd never run before. She would absolutely not get Thirteen — or me.

Miss Dupree came after me, shouting in a language I'd never heard. Her cats ran ahead of her and darted around and between my legs, trying to trip me. I kicked them away. With Thirteen clinging to my shoulders, I was unstoppable.

The rain hit the ground like BBs from an air rifle, and a jagged bolt of lightning flashed across the sky, leaping from one towering cloud to another.

I made it up the steps just ahead of Miss Dupree. She was so close I heard her gasping for breath. Sure that she'd grab me at any moment, I opened the front door, dashed inside, and slammed it shut. With shaking fingers, I bolted it against her.

Miss Dupree pounded on the door. "Give me my cat! You have no idea how sorry you'll be if you don't!"

Terrified, I dashed upstairs and locked Thirteen and me in my bedroom. The cat rubbed against my legs and purred so loudly she almost drowned out Miss Dupree's shouts.

I sank down on the floor beside Thirteen. She climbed into my lap, rested her paws on my shoulders, and rubbed her face against mine.

"I don't know how I got away from her," I told the cat. "She was so close I thought she'd grab you like she did before." I shut my eyes and shook so hard my bones rattled.

Thirteen stared at me with shining eyes and purred.

"You know I saved you, don't you?"

She purred louder and licked my nose.

Slowly I relaxed. The hammering on the door had stopped. I hoped Miss Dupree had gone home and taken her hideous cats with her.

I stroked Thirteen's skinny sides. My second encounter with Miss Dupree had been worse than my first. I stretched out my hand. It was still shaking and my heart was thumping hard.

"Do you think she's gone?" I whispered to Thirteen.

She stretched and went to the window. Standing on her hind legs, she pushed the curtain aside with her nose, looked out, and hissed.

I crept to her side. "Did you understand what I just said?"

She gave me an inscrutable cat stare and turned her attention to the group outside.

Miss Dupree and the cats had retreated to the sidewalk in front of my aunt's house. The sky was even darker now. Rain puddled on the sidewalk and ran fast and muddy in the gutters.

A gust of wind loosened Miss Dupree's hair, and it blew around her face in a tangle of gray and white strands. The black scarf she wore around her neck whipped. Her red dress blew against her body and clung to her hipbones. She didn't seem to notice the rain or her wet clothes. Raising her long thin white arms, she pointed at me.

"You!" she screamed. "*Zoey!* You'll be sorry you defied me. You have no idea who I am or what I can do!"

I slammed the window shut and closed the curtains. A torrent of rain struck the glass. Thunder boomed as if a wild animal crouched on the roof, roaring at the storm.

Scooping up Thirteen, I held her close. Her heart beat faster than mine and she trembled.

"She'll never get you," I whispered. "Never."

I pulled back a corner of the curtain and looked out. Miss Dupree and the cats were gone. The street was a river. Small branches and leaves floated past, spinning in the current. Trees swayed, their branches flailing in the wind. The rain fell so heavily I could barely see Lila's house.

"Who is she, Thirteen?" I whispered. "*What* is she? Did she bring the storm?"

A bolt of lightning plunged from the clouds to the ground and thunder boomed again.

I backed away from the window, and the cat pressed her face under my arm. "Lila was right," I whispered. "It's impossible, but she really is a witch. She must be."

Thirteen meowed and laid her ears back, just as if she was saying, *Yes, she is a witch, that's why I ran away.*

I held the cat tighter. Here I was, an ordinary girl in an ordinary room. My books on a shelf, my sandals under the bed, Aunt Alice's watercolors hanging on the walls. The house, the yard, the flowers—all ordinary.

But next door—the woods, the boarded-up house, the cats, the woman. They didn't belong here in the everyday world of Bexhill.

It was wrong, so wrong. So crazy scary wrong. What was her plan to make me sorry? How was I to defend myself against her?

I sat on the bed and hugged myself to keep from shaking. Thirteen looked at me long and hard and rubbed her face against my cheek.

"You know everything, don't you? If only you could tell me."

She meowed and meowed again, louder this time. Sadder too. Just as I thought the cat might actually speak, I heard the front door open.

I leapt up, terrified. Miss Dupree! She'd come back. She was in the house.

Where was my phone? It should have been in my pocket. I searched frantically, first my pockets, then under the bed—but then I remembered. I'd left my phone downstairs on the charger.

I heard her footsteps in the hall, the living room, the kitchen. Miss Dupree was walking around downstairs, looking for me. At any minute, she'd come upstairs, she'd force my door open, she'd take Thirteen, and she'd do something unimaginably horrible to me.

While I was trying to hide under my bed, a voice called, "Zoey, I'm home. Where are you?"

I lay on the floor, half under my bed. Aunt Alice was downstairs, not Miss Dupree. I was safe. I began crying like I'd never stop.

6

"ZOEY, ARE YOU IN THERE?" Aunt Alice jiggled my door handle. "Why is the door locked? Are you all right?"

I got to my feet and opened the door.

Aunt Alice stared at my face. "Oh my lord, you're crying." Pulling me close, she hugged me. "What's upset you so?"

"Oh, oh," I sobbed. "It's Miss Dupree. She — she —"

"Not her again. Didn't I tell you —"

"I didn't mean to, Aunt Alice. Thirteen escaped and the other cats chased her across the street. I found her under Lila's porch, but when I tried to bring her home, Miss Dupree came after me. She was right behind me, but I got inside. She pounded on the door and screamed at me. I was so scared."

Aunt Alice held me tighter. "I have a mind to go over there and tell her she can't get away with that sort of behavior. I won't tolerate it! How dare she frighten you like that and all because of one small cat!"

"No, don't go to her house. Don't ever go there."

"That woman can't scare me. The worst she can do is yell at me."

"You don't understand." I held her hands and stared at her. "She isn't just a weird old woman. She's, she's . . ." I couldn't bring myself to say it.

"Zoey, Zoey, dear Zoey." Aunt Alice squeezed my hands. "Miss Dupree isn't a witch. But perhaps we should treat her as if she is. We'll both stay away from her — and her cats."

At that moment, Thirteen crawled out from under the bed and rubbed against Aunt Alice's legs.

I snatched her up and held her so tightly she squirmed. "I am so not giving this cat back!"

Aunt Alice studied Thirteen. "The poor little thing. She looks like she's starving."

Thirteen meowed her tiny little meow and clung to my T-shirt with her claws.

"She's been treated very badly." Aunt Alice gently stroked Thirteen's side. "I can feel every rib. She's so malnourished that it's stunted her growth."

"And yet she's so sweet," I whispered. "Look at the way she cuddles in my arms. If Miss Dupree gets her, she'll starve her to death."

"I see what you mean," Aunt Alice murmured. "We have to keep her. That woman doesn't deserve to have this cat — or any cat."

My knees gave way and I sank down on my bed, in tears again. "Did you hear that, Thirteen? You're going to live with us. You'll be safe from that witch and her horrible cats."

"She must be so hungry," Aunt Alice said. "Let's take her downstairs and feed her."

While we watched Thirteen gobble canned tuna, I asked Aunt Alice, "What's a good name for a black cat?"

"Certainly not Thirteen," she said. "Not Blackie. Not Sable, not Ebony. She needs an unusual name—mysterious, magical, musical."

"A long time ago, I read a book about a girl named Nia who was abandoned in a forest when she was a baby," I told Aunt Alice. "A group of cats raised her along with their own kittens. Nia grew up thinking she was a cat too. I don't remember the title or how it ended, but I always loved the name Nia."

"Nia." Aunt Alice smiled. "Nia, yes, it's the perfect name for our mysterious black cat."

"How would you like to be called Nia?" I asked the cat. "It's much prettier than Thirteen."

She looked up from the tuna and touched my hand with her dainty paw. She seemed to agree it was the perfect name for her.

After Nia finished eating, Aunt Alice watched her groom herself. "I can't help wondering why Miss Dupree is so anxious to get her back. She has at least a dozen cats. You'd think she wouldn't even notice when one goes missing."

I hadn't thought about that. To me Nia was totally special. Of course Miss Dupree wanted her back. The other cats were mean and hateful and ugly. If one of them disappeared, I was sure she wouldn't miss it.

"We might never know why that woman thinks you're special," Aunt Alice told Nia. "But you're special to us because you're sweet and mysterious. You see and hear things that we know nothing about. We hope you stay with us for a very long time."

"She's not going anywhere. Right, Nia?" I kissed her nose and she purred.

"You know what?" Aunt Alice asked. "We need to go shopping for her. She needs cat food, a litterbox, litter, maybe a few toys." She smiled at Nia. "Anything else, my lady?"

Nia leapt into my aunt's lap and purred. "It's just as if she's thanking me!"

"Maybe she is." I reached out to stroke her head. "You're magical. That's why Miss Dupree wants you so much."

"I can almost believe that," Aunt Alice said.

Before I went to bed that night, I texted Lila and told her about Nia and my close call with Miss Dupree. "U shoulda been there, so scary, so witchy, u might be right bout her being a witch."

"OMG," she texted back. "ur amazing. luv her new name!!! be careful. library tomorrow see u day after."

I texted some funny witch GIFs to Lila and turned off my phone. Nia snuggled on the bed beside me. With her purring in my ear, I fell asleep quickly and easily and didn't wake up till morning.

After Aunt Alice left for the library, Nia roamed around the house and rubbed against furniture as if to say, *Mine. Mine. Mine.* When she'd established ownership of everything in the house, she played with the catnip mouse Aunt Alice had bought on her trip to the store for cat food and litter. She knocked it across the floor, stopping now and then to pounce on it. She rolled on it, chewed it, tossed it up in the air, caught it, and then tried to disembowel it. I hoped I'd never see her treat a living mouse like that.

Suddenly she lost interest in the mouse, jumped on the back of the sofa, and looked out the window. The cats had lined up on our porch railing. When they saw Nia, they leapt to the windowsill, pressed their faces against the screen, and hissed.

Nia arched her back and spat. Oh, she was a fierce one—smaller than any of the others, but now that she was inside and they were outside, she wasn't afraid.

More scared than she was, I yelled, "Shoo, scat, get away from here!"

Instead of leaving, the cats hooked their sharp claws in the screen as if they meant to tear a hole big enough to get through. The largest one clung to the screen with all four sets of claws and yowled like a savage beast.

I slammed down the window and closed the curtains, but they stayed on the sill and tore at the screen. It was like that old movie *The Birds,* only with cats. Except it wasn't a movie. It was for real.

All of a sudden, the noise stopped. In the silence, I heard a knock on the door. Someone had come to the house and frightened the cats away. Lila — *it must be Lila!* She hadn't gone to the library after all. I ran to let her in before the cats came back.

But it wasn't Lila's smiling face I saw. Before I could slam the door shut, Miss Dupree pushed me aside and stormed into the living room. She looked scarier than ever. Her hair had escaped the bun and straggled over her shoulders. Her black-and-red-striped dress was wrinkled and her matching scarf was untied.

I backed away from her, both terrified and angry. "Get out of here! You can't just barge into my aunt's house. I'll call the police."

I grabbed my phone, but before I could touch the keypad, Miss Dupree knocked it out of my hand.

We were face-to-face now, close enough for me to smell the musty odor of unwashed skin and hair. "I've come for Thirteen. The sooner you hand her over, the sooner I'll be gone."

"She's not here," I lied. "Aunt Alice gave her to a friend who wanted a cat."

Miss Dupree curled her lip the way a dog does when it's about to bite. "Don't lie to me. Fetch Thirteen — now!"

I flinched and took another step backward. "I can't give you what I don't have."

Turning to the open door, Miss Dupree called, "Number One, come, my dear. I need your help."

The white Persian ran into the house. "Find Thirteen," Miss Dupree said. "Bring her to me. I'm fed up with this girl's lies and thievery."

Number One ran straight to the kitchen. Desperate to protect Nia, I forgot my fear and ran after her. "She's gone," I cried. "She's not here!" I waved my arms. "Scat, scat!"

Ignoring me, the white cat crouched down and crept toward the cabinet in the corner. She shoved her nose under it, but she was too big to wedge herself into the small space. Her bushy tail whipped back and forth. She growled. Her teeth chattered like Suki's when she watched birds fly past a window.

"Get away from there!" I shoved her with my foot, and she yowled at me.

"Don't you dare kick my cat!" Miss Dupree pushed me so hard I fell over a chair and landed on the floor.

Dropping to her knees beside Number One, Miss Dupree reached under the cabinet and fumbled about in the darkness. Her fingernails clicked across the floor like claws.

"She's close," Miss Dupree snarled. "I smell her. Where have you hidden her?"

"I already told you." My voice shook with fear. "My aunt gave her away."

Miss Dupree got up slowly, as if her knees hurt. "All right, Zoey," she wheezed. "You might think you've fooled me, but I'm much smarter than you realize. You won't trick me again. I want that cat and I'll get her. You'll see."

Her voice trailed off in a fit of coughing, and she leaned against the table for a moment before heading for the door. Number One hissed at me and followed Miss Dupree outside. I slammed the door behind them and made sure to turn the bolt.

"Nia," I called. "Where are you?"

Nothing moved in the shadows under the cabinet, but I heard a faint scrabbling sound coming from inside. I opened the door and Nia trotted out. She looked very proud of herself. Rising on her haunches, she touched my face gently with her paw and began to purr.

I held her close and pressed my face against her soft black fur. "How did you get inside that cabinet? Did you learn magic from Miss Dupree?"

She looked at me with her big round eyes and purred louder. Maybe she really had picked up a few tricks from Miss Dupree. But then she squirmed out of my arms and walked off to use her litterbox. *She's just a cat,* I thought, *but a very smart one.*

By the time Aunt Alice came home, I'd decided not to tell her about Miss Dupree's visit. This time, she'd really go straight next door and make a scene of some kind. If she made Miss Dupree mad, there was no telling what the witch would do.

But I texted Lila every detail and ended it with "Ur so right, witch for real. Scared, come over tomorrow."

The next morning, I followed Aunt Alice to the porch and asked for a hug before she left for work. After my third meeting with Miss Dupree, I was kind of clingy. Scared too. What if she came back today and did something worse?

"Look," Aunt Alice said. "The cats are gone!"

I stared at the fence. Not a cat in sight. "Where are they?"

Aunt Alice smiled. "Maybe they've finally found somewhere else to go." Giving me another big hug, she said, "You and Lila have a nice day."

I sat on the railing and watched her walk away. Up the street, a man mowed his lawn. Two women jogged by. Across the street, a UPS truck stopped, and the driver left an Amazon box on someone's porch. A dog barked. Such a normal street, such an ordinary morning. It was amazing how little people knew about their own neighborhood and the people who lived near them.

While I waited for Lila, I worried about Miss Dupree's threat to make me sorry. Sooner or later, she'd move against me. I didn't know what she'd do or when she'd do it, but I was sure witches didn't make idle threats. Something bad was going to happen. Maybe not today, maybe not tomorrow, but soon. I felt it coming.

Lila called to me and I looked up to see her running across the street. She flopped into the swing beside me. "Where are the cats? It's so weird not to see them lined up on the fence like Halloween."

"I don't know." I looked around, but they weren't in sight.

"They could be anywhere," Lila said. "Like under the porch right now, listening to everything we say. Or up on the roof or who knows where. They're a witch's cats, after all."

Nia meowed and Lila turned to see her at the window. Jumping out of the swing, she pressed her nose against the screen. "Hi, Nia. I'm Lila, Zoey's friend. You're the prettiest cat I ever saw.

Even if you did belong to a witch—which is so totally not your fault."

Nia rubbed her side against the screen and purred. Lila grinned at me. "She likes me."

"That's because we're friends."

Lila sat down beside me again and the swing swayed. "I'm sorry I wasn't home yesterday to help you. I can't imagine that woman in my house." She shuddered. "Ugh. It makes my skin crawl to think of it."

"I wish you'd been here. Poor Nia and I were so scared."

Lila looked me in the eye. "But you believe she's a witch now, right?"

"It's the only explanation. She got down on her knees and sniffed under the cupboard like an animal. She smelled Nia. It was gross."

"Why did you open the door?"

"I thought it was you."

Lila rocked the swing and bit her fingernails. "Did you tell your aunt?"

"Not this time. I don't want her to go over there and make a scene and get cursed or something."

"Yeah, I can see your aunt doing that. She's pretty feisty." Lila gnawed at her thumb. "Are you still scared?"

"Well, yeah, sort of. I have this feeling something bad is going to happen, like a big dark cloud hanging over me. Do you know what I mean?"

Lila nodded. "I get in those moods too, but most of the time nothing happens."

"I've never had one like this."

A little silence fell then. We swayed back and forth, barely moving. We just didn't have the energy to send the swing flying.

I heard footsteps coming toward the house. Fearing it was Miss Dupree, I looked up quickly.

"Lila," I whispered. "Who's that?"

A young woman strolled toward us. Her hair was long and blond, silvery in the sunlight. She wore black slacks and a gauzy, low-cut black tunic. Her high-heeled sandals were red. The leather purse slung over her shoulder was also red, and the large drawing portfolio under her arm was black.

What was someone like her doing in Bexhill? She belonged with the fashionable women in New York, the ones who walked as if they owned the city.

To my surprise, she stopped and smiled. "Hello," she called. "I don't believe I've met either of you. I'm Zleta Delgata. Your neighbor, Miss Dupree, is my beloved aunt."

We stared at her, speechless. How could such a beautiful young woman be Miss Dupree's niece?

"May I join you for a moment?" Her slight accent made her all the more glamorous.

I nodded, amazed that someone so glamorous would want to sit on a porch with Lila and me.

"You must be Zoey," she said to me. "My aunt has told me about you, the girl next door."

She turned to ask Lila her name, leaving me to worry about what Miss Dupree had told Miss Delgata. It couldn't have been anything good, that was for sure.

For the first time since I'd met her, Lila seemed unsure of herself. She murmured her name in such a low voice that Miss Delgata asked her to say it again.

"I'm happy to meet you girls." She took a seat in the swing between Lila and me. Pushing lightly with her feet, she made it sway slightly. "Ah, so lovely, so old-fashioned, this swing. So comfortable."

Lila finally spoke up. "Are you an artist, Miss Delgata?"

"Please call me Zleta," she said. "I'm not one for formality."

She touched her portfolio. "Have you heard of the famous fashion designer Madame Eugenie?"

We shook our heads.

"You'll be surprised to hear she lives next door to you. Yes, it's true. My aunt is Madame Eugenie! She's so shy, poor dear, so introverted. She keeps herself to herself and tells no one what she does. But you must have noticed the beautiful clothes she wears."

"Everyone wonders where she buys them," Lila said. "They look so expensive."

"Oh, yes, it's a pity that so few can afford her fashions. Only the very wealthy, you know. Because I'm her assistant, it's my good fortune to wear her clothing." Zleta stood up and spun around to show off her outfit.

"If she's so rich and famous," I said, "why does she live in that old, falling-down house?"

Lila looked at me as if I'd asked a rude question, but I was just trying to make sense of what Zleta told us. If I were rich and famous, I'd live in a mansion with beautiful views and lots of flowers and sunshine. On a cliff above the Pacific Ocean maybe. Certainly not in a house like Miss Dupree's.

"Aunt has no need for mansions, Zoey. Her seclusion allows her to work undisturbed." Zleta patted the portfolio. "The drawings for next summer's designs are in here, with comments from her agent. Aunt doesn't allow the public to see them before the season opens, but I'll give you girls a sneak peek."

I glanced at the fence to see if the cats were watching, but they still hadn't appeared in their usual places. Their absence made me nervous. Zleta made me nervous.

She opened her portfolio and spread out several drawings of dresses and other fashionable outfits. Some were sketches in black ink, others were watercolor, and they were all beautiful.

"Did Miss Dupree draw these?" Lila asked.

"Oh, yes. She's extremely talented." Zleta reached over and touched Lila's hair. "Such a lovely color, so thick and shiny. And your face." She cupped her hands in a heart shape. "Have you ever thought about a modeling career? Young girls of your type are much in demand now." She stepped back and studied Lila.

"You have the perfect build. Slender. Long legs. Expressive eyes and a sweet mouth."

"Me? A model?" Lila laughed. "Are you kidding? I'm way too clumsy. I'd fall off the runway or something and ruin the show."

"Oh, no, no. We can fix clumsy." Zleta laughed. "You are what, fourteen? Fifteen? Just the right age! Think about it. I can arrange headshots by a professional photographer and introduce you to the right people."

"I'm only twelve," Lila stammered. "And I have school. My parents would never . . . No, I can't, but I wish . . ." She stared at Zleta as if she'd been enchanted.

"If you change your mind, darling, let me know. I hate to see a beautiful girl miss an opportunity to be on the cover of *Vogue.* To walk the runways in Milan, Paris, Rome. A top model." She opened her purse and drew out a business card. "Please, consider the financial success that can be yours. Your parents will be impressed by the money you'll earn."

Lila took the card and studied it. "Thank you," she whispered. "Thank you, Zleta."

Zleta swung her head toward me, and I noticed how sweet her hair smelled, like roses or lilacs or something. "And you, little Miss Zoey. Aunt told me about the terrible misunderstanding between you. All because of one insignificant cat. She regrets losing her temper and coming to your house uninvited. She said things she didn't mean and wishes to apologize for her behavior. She's really a sweet and kind woman, Zoey, but that cat means a great deal to her. She cannot bear its loss. She hopes you'll visit her to see what can be worked out. Do you think we can arrange that?"

No, I thought, *definitely not. Your aunt scares me to death. Not to mention that she's a witch.* Out loud, I said, "My aunt told me to stay away from Miss Dupree."

"Aunt is peculiar and often rude, but it's her artistic temperament. And sometimes, you know, when a person spends too much time alone, she forgets how to socialize with others. But under it all, Aunt has a kind heart, Zoey, you'll see."

I studied my running shoes, brand-new this summer, the kind everybody wore. Zleta's belief in her aunt was pitiful. Miss Dupree did not have a kind heart. Even her fingernails were cruel and sharp and hurtful. I'd never go near her house. I'd never agree to return Nia. Never.

Zleta gathered up the sketches and put them into her portfolio. "I've enjoyed meeting you girls. I hope you'll both accept what I've offered you."

Lila and I watched her walk away. Taking a key from her purse, she unlocked Miss Dupree's gate. The cats ran out of the bushes to greet her. They rubbed against her legs and purred as if they were normal everyday cats. Then, following close behind her, they disappeared into the trees.

Lila looked at me. "Would you ever have guessed Miss Dupree is a famous fashion designer?"

"No, not in a million years. Whoever heard of a witch doing anything but witchiness?"

"Maybe we were wrong about her," Lila said. "Surely Zleta

would know if her aunt was a witch. She never even hinted at anything like that."

"Don't you think Zleta's kind of strange?" I struggled to say what bothered me. "It's her *eyes*," I said. "They're the same weird color as Miss Dupree's eyes."

"So? They're related. Why shouldn't their eyes be the same color?"

"It's not only the color. It's the way she looked at me. I swear she read my mind just like Miss Dupree. Didn't you notice? Or were you too flattered by the modeling stuff to see?"

"Are you jealous because Zleta thinks I should be a model?"

"Of course not! You could definitely be a model. I just don't trust Zleta." Even though I knew I was making Lila angry, I didn't back off. "How can you believe anything a relative of Miss Dupree says? You can't trust Zleta — not what she said about Miss Dupree and not what she said about your so-called modeling career."

"You *are* jealous," Lila said. "Zleta didn't say *you* should be a model. She didn't say *you* were beautiful! She didn't say anything about you except to give back Nia!" Lila ran down the steps and across the street to her house. Without looking back, she let the door slam behind her.

I sat alone on the swing, both sad and mad. I should have kept my mouth shut, but no, not me. I blabbed and blabbed about Zleta and Miss Dupree. And now I'd lost my only friend in Bexhill.

But what kind of friend was Lila? A few compliments from

Miss Dupree's niece had changed everything. She trusted Zleta now, not me.

I got to my feet, almost too tired to move, and went inside. Nia met me at the door and rubbed against my legs as if to comfort me. She led me to the kitchen, where she sat down beside her empty dish and looked at me.

I opened the cat food. "See? I know what you want even if you can't tell me."

7

AFTER I ATE A peanut butter and banana sandwich, washed down with lemonade, I sat at Aunt Alice's computer and typed *Eugenie Dupree* in the search box. I'd find out if she was a famous fashion designer. Which I doubted very much. Then I'd convince Lila to trust me, not Zleta.

In seconds, I was stunned to see a ton of hits—Pinterest, Instagram, Twitter, Wikipedia, and, of course, Madame Eugenie's webpage. Photographs showed Miss Dupree and Zleta in Rome, London, Berlin, and Paris, always smiling, always dressed in Madame Eugenie's fashions. Zleta's hair and makeup were perfect, and Miss Dupree looked suave and sophisticated, a stylish older woman, often wearing sunglasses.

I scrolled through pages of models dressed in Miss Dupree's creations. They were very young, very thin, and very pretty. Some were white, some Black, some Asian. They posed as if they'd been told to look angry or sulky. They pouted, they frowned, they glared. With their spindly legs and arms, they looked like homeless orphans.

Lila was much prettier than any of them.

The next day, I sat on the porch all by myself. No cats watched me from the fence. Aunt Alice was at the library and so was Lila. My only company was Nia. She slept on the windowsill, stretched out gracefully, seemingly totally relaxed but, like all cats, she was ready to wake up and run if she had to.

Yesterday's bad feeling hung over me, darkening my mood. I tried to escape it by reading, but my thoughts strayed from Camelot to the house next door and the witch who hid in its shadows. What was she planning? Was Zleta still there, or had she gone back to the city?

I rocked the swing gently, my book forgotten. Why had Zleta spent so much time with Lila and me yesterday? Why had she tried to talk Lila into becoming a model? All that gushing, all those compliments—not that Lila wasn't pretty. She was, but it was as if Zleta wanted to take Lila away from me and use her in some way.

Nia scratched on the window screen and mewed. I wished she and I were sitting on the swing together, but I didn't dare bring her outside. Luckily she showed no sign of wanting to leave the house.

My thoughts went back to Lila. Let her think what she pleased, but I wasn't jealous. My issue was Zleta, not Lila's looks. Something wasn't right about Miss Dupree's niece, but I couldn't say what it was—just that it was hidden much better than Miss Dupree's wrongness.

I looked at Lila's house. Later this afternoon, when she came home from the library, maybe she'd come over. We'd make up and be friends again. I'd convince her I wasn't jealous. I'd tell her not to trust Zleta. I'd show her Dupree's website and the pitiful, half-starved models.

I picked up my book again, determined to keep my mind on Arthur and Merlyn. There was danger in Camelot, but it was safe danger locked in a book. It wasn't right next door in the real world.

Zleta joined me so quietly, I didn't notice her until she said hello. It was almost as if she'd magicked herself out of the air.

"I didn't mean to startle you, Zoey. Aunt says I'm as quiet as a cat."

Without waiting to be asked, she sat beside me. I moved as far away from her as the swing allowed. If she'd come with another invitation to visit her aunt, she'd be disappointed.

"You look so cute this morning, Zoey," she said. "The blue T-shirt matches your eyes."

She looked nice in her beige cropped trousers and white shirt, but I didn't tell her. She already knew she was beautiful.

Zleta smiled and leaned toward me. "I told Aunt I met you. She hopes you'll visit her soon so she can apologize for the way she treated you." She sighed and swept her hair to one side, releasing the sweet scent of her shampoo. Leaning closer, she said, "Truly, Aunt has gotten a bit cranky in her old age. I worry about her living alone with those cats. They're so precious to her, but they aren't nice cats, as I'm sure you've noticed."

She leaned a little closer. "Aunt is old. Her heart has known more sorrow than you in your youth can imagine. I beg you to return Thirteen, as she calls her. She's her favorite cat, the only one who sits in her lap and purrs, the only one who enjoys being petted and kissed and loved."

As Zleta talked, I relaxed. Perhaps Lila was right, and I was wrong about Zleta. It wasn't her fault that she was related to Miss Dupree. Her voice was so soft and pleasant, and she smelled so nice. I was glad to have all her attention. If Lila were here, they'd be talking about modeling and I'd be left out.

"My poor aunt. So lonely. So sad. Not a friend in this town." Zleta sighed. Her breath tickled my ear, and I moved closer to her, so close my shoulder touched hers.

"Your shampoo," I murmured, "it smells so nice. Where do you get it? I'd love to have some."

Zleta smiled and shook her head, releasing waves of fragrance. "It's made especially for me by a dear friend of my aunt. Very costly. Believe me, you couldn't pay the price she asks."

I rested my head on her shoulder and breathed deeply. "Mmmmm. I'll have to smell yours then."

Giddy, I was so giddy. And dizzy. Giddy and dizzy, dizzy and giddy. I started giggling, and for a minute I couldn't stop. Embarrassed, I moved back to my side of the swing. The fragrance faded and I yawned.

Somewhere in the back of my head an alarm buzzed faintly, but I ignored it. Lila trusted Zleta. I trusted Zleta. Why not?

"Now, about Thirteen," Zleta said softly. "What's the chief reason you won't return her to Aunt Eugenie?"

I had to think before I answered. Why had I stolen Nia from the poor old woman next door? Why did I hold on to her when Miss Dupree needed her so much? What a selfish person I was. And a thief too. It was suddenly clear that I must return Nia. It was the right thing to do.

Behind me, Nia scratched the screen and meowed. The fog in my head cleared. I sat up straight. Without realizing it, I'd moved closer to Zleta. I slid away from her again. If only she'd leave — I wanted to go inside and play with Nia, but that would be rude.

"I don't believe that Nia ever sat in your aunt's lap," I said. "She hates Miss Dupree. That's why she tried to run away over and over again. I rescued her. I saved her! I'll never give her back!"

Zleta looked past me at Nia. Her eyes narrowed, and Nia jumped down from the windowsill and disappeared from sight.

"So *that* is Thirteen," she said softly. "I see why Aunt wants her back. A cat like that, so perfect, her coat so shiny, her tail so full."

"Her name is *Nia*," I said. "You should have seen her when I rescued her. She was lots skinnier and her coat was sort of dull, like she never got good quality cat food. If your aunt loved her so much, why didn't she take better care of her?"

Zleta looked at me as if I'd hurt her deeply. "Oh, Zoey, how can you say Aunt didn't take good care of Thirteen?"

"Her name is Nia," I said. "Nia. Thirteen is a number, not a name."

"Thirteen, Nia, whatever." Zleta slid close to me again. The fragrance of her hair surrounded me like a delicious cloud. I tried to move away from her, to get up and go inside with Nia, but my body liked being where it was.

"I understand your anger," she murmured. "You love Thirteen so much. You don't want to give her up, so you pretend the cat was unhappy with Aunt."

"She *was* unhappy." I shifted my weight in the swing. The seat's wooden slats felt hard and uncomfortable.

"But you must see Aunt loves Thirteen just as much you do. And *she* owns the cat, not you."

"No one owns a cat." I swatted at the air to clear my head, but the perfume clung to my hair and my skin. My mind was muzzy again, slow.

"How about this?" Zleta smoothed my hair. "What if Aunt has found a cat who's just as sweet as Thirteen? Would you trade?"

Somehow Zleta had won me back to her side. I wanted to please her. I wanted to be her friend. I wanted her to tell me I was just as beautiful as Lila and I could be a famous model too. Most of all, I wanted her to like me better than Lila.

But I loved Nia too. "Why can't your aunt keep the other cat and let me keep Nia?"

"Please, Zoey. Aunt needs Thirteen."

"I need her too." I was close to tears. I didn't want to argue with Zleta, but I couldn't give Nia back to Miss Dupree. I simply could not do it.

Zleta stood up as gracefully as a ballerina. Her hair swirled around her perfect face. "Please come to my aunt's house and tell her how you feel. She has a tender heart, you know, a kindness that she often hides. Perhaps she'll let you keep Thirteen. Wouldn't that be nice?"

I shrank from the hand she offered. "No, I don't want to talk to her." The truth was I was so tired, so very tired, much too tired to visit Miss Dupree.

"I see. You're afraid of her, aren't you?"

"No," I said. But I couldn't look her in the eye and lie, so I corrected myself. "Yes," I whispered. "I'm afraid of her."

"But I'll be with you. Surely you aren't afraid of me."

A breeze fanned Zleta's hair. I took her hand and let her help me to my feet.

"Of course I'm not afraid of you," I whispered. "You're the most beautiful person I've ever met."

She smiled. "You're so sweet. I believe you'll be a better model than Lila. You have a special quality. A sort of naivete that appeals to me. After you and Aunt come to an agreement, we'll discuss your fashion career."

I let Zleta lead me away from Aunt Alice's house. I trusted her now. She thought I was beautiful. I might even be a better model than Lila. I had a quality she lacked, but I couldn't remember what it was. Maybe I was nicer.

Behind me, I heard Nia meow and meow, again and again, as

if she was calling me back. I hesitated. Maybe I shouldn't go with Zleta, but the grip of her soft hand was too strong to break.

Zleta unlocked Miss Dupree's gate. After that, I didn't hear Nia. I let Zleta lead me down a narrow path that seemed to be several miles long. I was trapped in a cloud of perfume and silvery-blond hair. Everything except Zleta was far away and unimportant.

We stopped at the front door. It was tall and painted black. The knocker was a ferocious cat's head cast in iron. In its mouth was an iron ring. It was the scariest cat I'd ever seen.

Zleta touched the knocker. "Beautiful, isn't it?" She smiled again, and I noticed how big and white her teeth were.

"Don't be worried, Zoey. Please believe me, Aunt regrets her harsh words to you. She hopes to befriend you."

I thought she added softly, "But only if you return her cat."

She opened the door and we went inside. After the bright sunlight, the house was so dark I couldn't see anything. Barely visible, the black cats stepped out of the shadows and gathered around me as if to keep me from leaving. I looked behind me, expecting to see Zleta.

In her place, Miss Dupree stood looking at me. "Welcome to my home, my dear Zoey. I've been expecting you."

"Where's Zleta?" I asked. "She promised to stay with me."

"I sent her to fetch you. Now that you're here, I no longer need her." She took my arm. Her fingers were cold and her grip was tight. "Let's go to the parlor and have a nice little chat about my cat."

I tried to resist, but I felt like I'd just run two or three laps around the exercise field at school. Maybe if I sat down and rested, I'd have the strength to go home.

Dim light sifted into the room through gaps in the plywood covering the windows. From what I could see, everything in the parlor was painted black—walls, ceiling, fireplace, furniture. Even the carpet was black. It reminded me of some artist Mom liked, but I couldn't remember her name.

Miss Dupree seated me on a small black sofa, so hard it might have been a church pew. She sat across from me in a chair that looked as uncomfortable as the sofa. Some of the cats nestled near Miss Dupree, but the others squeezed themselves onto the sofa with me. Not to sit in my lap, not to be petted, but to make sure I stayed exactly where Miss Dupree wanted me.

The room smelled like Zleta's hair: thick, rich, sweet. Every time I took a breath, I felt weaker.

"I have given some thought to the problem of the cat you call Nia." She leaned toward me and stared into my eyes. "If you return her, I'll give you another cat in place of her. A much prettier cat, a sweeter cat. You can choose any color, any breed."

"I don't want another cat. I just want Nia." My voice had begun to shake with fatigue. Keeping my eyes open was almost impossible. "Why can't *you* get another cat and let Nia stay with me?"

She narrowed her eyes to slits. "I need the cat in ways you don't understand."

"I won't give her to you. You'll hurt her." Despite my efforts, my speech slowed down like an old-fashioned music box. My eyelids were weighted with exhaustion. *I must not fall asleep in this house,* I told myself. *I must not.* The perfumed air filled my lungs. *If only I could go home. If only . . . only, only . . .*

"I have ways to get what I want, Zoey. You'll see. Oh yes, indeed you will. I will get the cat and you will pay for your insolence." Miss Dupree's voice came from far away, but I understood every word.

"Who are you, what do . . . why . . ."

Although I couldn't express myself clearly, Miss Dupree understood me. She leaned closer, her crazy witchy eyes boring into mine.

"I have a score to settle with you, dear Zoey. Your obstinacy made me lose control of myself. I brawled in the street with you. I chased you home. I shouted at you from the sidewalk. You made me reveal myself in public, something a witch must never do. Your fault, all of it. If you had just given me that blasted cat, you would not be here with me."

Her voice was muffled now and distorted. "Once you did not know who I was, once you did not know what I can do. Now you have become a danger to me. I cannot allow you to leave my house."

The perfume grew stronger. The room grew darker. Smaller. It was hard to breathe, difficult to think, impossible to understand Miss Dupree's garbled words. I gave up trying to struggle. I no longer cared where I was or what happened to me. I closed my eyes and let go. Sleep was all I wanted.

8

WHEN I WOKE, I was curled up on the same hard black
sofa. I tried to sit up, but the best I could do was crouch
on my hands and knees. My body wasn't behaving like itself at
all. I ached all over. My very bones hurt. I tried to push myself up
and managed to sit on my haunches.

That's when I saw my furry black paws. My chest and abdo-
men were covered with black fur. In disbelief, I examined every
part of me, but all I saw was black fur. At the end of my spine was
a long black tail. Touching a paw to my face, I felt whiskers and
a damp, cold nose. My ears sat on top of my head instead of on
the sides.

No. It had to be a dream, a nightmare. I couldn't be a cat.
It was impossible. I was a girl. Zoey was my name. I was twelve
years old.

Wake up, Zoey, I begged myself. *Wake up.* I shook my head. I
widened my eyes as if they might still be closed. I bit myself. But
nothing changed.

I tried standing like a human being, tottered a few steps, lost
my balance, and fell. The only way to move was to use four legs.

With my belly pressed to the floor, I ran around the room, looking for a way to escape.

Why was the room so dark? Furniture, walls, floors, rugs—all black. No windows. There had to be a door, but I couldn't find it.

My heart pounded. I gulped air like I was drowning. There was no way out. I was trapped in this black room. In the body of a cat.

I'd been drugged. That was it—I was hallucinating. At any second, the drug would wear off and I'd be me again. Zoey. But where was I? Who had given me drugs?

Slowly, I remembered Zleta. Yes, Zleta, she'd drugged me, she'd brought me here. I hadn't wanted to come to this house, but Zleta, Zleta . . . I'd trusted her. She was beautiful, she was, she was . . . Who was she? Where was I? In despair, I crawled under a sofa and crouched close to the wall.

After a while, a door opened and let in a narrow beam of daylight. Three black cats crept into the room. I cowered under the sofa. I'd seen them before. Somewhere. I didn't know where. On a fence maybe. They meant to hurt me. I was afraid of them.

One poked her nose under the sofa. "Welcome," she said. "You're one of us now. A new sister."

How could it be that I understood her?

"Don't be scared," the cat said. "We won't hurt you. Not now that you're one of us."

I peeked out and saw the cats sitting on the floor watching me. They didn't look vicious, just curious.

"Where am I?" I whispered.

"In the witch's house," one said.

"What has she done to me?"

Another of the cats stretched out a paw and examined her claws. "What she's done to all of us."

"No more, no less," the third said.

My mind began to clear. I was in Miss Dupree's house. Zleta had brought me here. "Are you saying that Miss Dupree changed you into cats? That you used to be girls like me?"

The three looked at one another. "We don't remember much about before," said the first.

The second chimed in: "It seems so long ago. Sometimes I think I've never been anything but a cat."

"Yes, me too," the third cat said. "I used to dream about a woman tucking me into bed at night and kissing me, but I don't know who she is or why I woke up from that dream crying."

"She must be your mother. You lived with her before you came here," I said. "You had a name—"

"We don't have mothers," the cat answered, "but we have names. I'm Twelve. She's Eleven, and she's Ten."

"Those are numbers, not names. A real name is like mine—Zoey."

"We never had any other names," Eleven said.

"If we did, we don't remember them," Ten said.

"It's forbidden to remember them," Eleven added.

Twelve licked my face. "Don't worry. Mistress will give you a name like ours. You're the fourteenth cat, so you'll be called Fourteen."

"I won't answer unless you call me by my right name."

"You don't need that name now. You'll soon forget it."

"You'll forget your other life too. Your new life is here with us," said Eleven.

I backed away from them. "My life will never be here. It's with my aunt and my mother. I won't forget it, either!" I sat up on my haunches and glared at them. "That witch can't keep me here. I'll run away like——"

Twelve pressed her paw over my mouth. "No! No! Don't say her name! We do not speak of her!"

"Hush, all of you," Eleven whispered. "Mistress will hear. She'll punish us. We'll go to the dungeon."

Suddenly Ten's ears swiveled toward the door. "Listen."

The three cats drew closer together and looked at the door, ears up, alert as cats can be.

"Footsteps outside."

"On the sidewalk."

"Going past the house."

"No, coming here."

"Nobody comes here."

"Hide."

The cats herded me under the couch. "Don't move. Be still," said Twelve. They pressed around me and trembled with fear. "We shouldn't be with you. Mistress will send us to the dungeon."

It was the second time they mentioned a dungeon—what did they mean? Surely this house didn't have a real dungeon.

Before I could ask, someone knocked on the front door. The

cats pressed even closer to me, holding me still with the strength of their bodies.

"Not one squeak," Twelve hissed at me.

The house was silent, holding its breath, as if waiting for the visitor to give up and go away.

But the visitor knocked again, louder this time.

Finally, Miss Dupree, with Zleta by her side, tiptoed to the door and pressed her ear against it.

A series of loud and louder knocks pounded the door. "Zleta," a girl's voice called. "Open the door! I know you're in there!"

My whole body tightened like a fist. Why was Lila here? *Please go home,* I begged her silently. *Please do not come in. Go away, Lila, go away.*

"Open the door!" Lila shouted again. "Zoey's missing. The whole neighborhood is looking for her. I saw her go inside with you. Is she in there?"

Miss Dupree whispered to Zleta and scurried upstairs. Zleta opened the door. Lila stood on the porch trying to look past Zleta as if she might see me in the shadows behind her.

"No, no, Lila! Go away. Don't come in here!" My words came out of my mouth in a stream of meows.

The other cats piled on top of me. "Be quiet. Hush. Mistress will hear you!"

"Oh, my dear Lila," Zleta said. "Such frightening news. Yes, I brought Zoey here to visit Aunt. I'm happy to say they made up their differences and came to an agreement about the cat. Zoey promised to trade Thirteen for another cat just as nice as Thirteen is." Zleta laughed. "Problem solved!"

Go away, Lila. Please stay away from this house, I begged. Behind her, I glimpsed the evening sky. Somehow, while I'd been changing into a cat, the day had changed into night. It was way past dinnertime. Aunt Alice must be worried about me.

"Is Zoey still here?" Lila asked.

She had no idea what had happened to me in this house. If she didn't leave soon, she'd learn the hard way.

"Your friend left hours ago," Zleta said. "I don't know where she went. She didn't say." Taking Lila's hand, she drew her into the hall. "Come in, have a cup of tea with me. You look sick with worry."

Lila hesitated. "I should go home. My parents—"

Yes, yes, go home, Lila. Leave this place before it's too late.

"Surely your parents know you're just across the street." Zleta's voice was smooth as velvet but dangerous at the same time.

"Dad told me to stay home, but I sneaked out after he and Mom left to join the search party. I thought I'd find Zoey here and we'd go home together and surprise everyone."

Oh, Lila, why did you tell Zleta that? Now she knows your parents think you're safe at home. I wanted to scratch her with my new claws.

"No one saw you come here?" Zleta tipped her head to the side and her hair swung. The sweetness of her perfume tickled my nose.

"Nobody saw me. They think . . . they didn't . . . they . . . Oh, your perfume, so good, so sweet . . ."

Lila's speech was slowing down. The spaces between her words grew longer and she yawned twice.

"You're tired, dear Lila," Zleta murmured. "You need to rest."

"This house . . . so dark." Lila's voice wavered. "Shadows, no light. Home . . . I should . . . my mother . . . But you smell so good, you are . . ."

"Oh, Lila, sweet Lila, come sit with me on the sofa."

"Home," Lila murmured. "But so tired . . ." She tried to say more, but her words slid together and ran downhill into a muddle. She collapsed on the sofa, right over my head.

"Yes, yes, sleep now, Lila. Sleep."

Lulled by Zleta's sweet scent, my new friend fell into deep sleep. I struggled to stay awake, but my eyelids were so heavy, I couldn't keep them up, and I drifted away. The last thing I heard was a voice chanting in a strange, guttural language.

———

Lila's groans woke me. I crawled out of my hiding place and saw her tossing and turning on the sofa.

Black fur covered her body. She'd grown whiskers and a tail. Her body twisted and jerked as if she were having a fit. Before my eyes, her arms, her legs, her body changed shape violently. Human moans changed to growls. When the change was complete, Lila was gone. In her place, a black cat struggled to sit up.

I jumped onto the sofa. "Lila, it's me, Zoey. Don't be scared."

She blinked — surprised, I guess, to hear a cat talk. "Don't be ridiculous. You're not Zoey. You're a cat."

She stretched her leg, saw her paw, and screamed. "What's happened to my feet? They look like a cat's paws. There's black hair all over me!" She swatted furiously at her tail as if she might scare it away.

"Lila, listen to me. It's impossible, but it's true. Miss Dupree has changed us both into cats."

She shook her head and whimpered. "No, no. This is all a dream. Any minute now, I'll wake up in my own bed, like Dorothy. Remember? Oz and the wizard and everything that happened to her was a dream, and the Wicked Witch of the West was really Miss Gulch riding her bicycle down the road. It will be just like that. We'll be home and we'll be girls, and Miss Dupree will be the crazy cat lady."

The other three cats jumped onto the sofa with us. "Please don't talk so loud," Ten whispered to Lila. "Mistress hates loud voices. She'll put you in the dungeon."

Lila burrowed into my side and shook all over. "No, no, no. Wake me up, Zoey, please!"

"It's not a dream. You're not asleep." I lay beside her and licked her fur as if I were a mother cat soothing her kitten.

Lila closed her eyes and lay so still I thought she'd stopped breathing. "It won't be forever, though. She'll change us back, right?"

I looked at my three new friends.

"Yes, of course. She'll change you into a girl every night," Eleven said. "But you won't like it."

"What do you mean?" Lila asked.

"She makes us sew all night long," said Twelve. "It's hard and boring and Number One watches us to make sure we do everything right and don't talk to each other."

"But in the daytime," Ten said, "we get to be cats again. We play in the woods and catch mice and do as we please. It's much more fun than being a girl."

"Yes, we catch mice and birds and bite their heads off and eat them." Twelve licked her lips.

"Bluebirds taste best," Eleven said.

"Hummingbirds are even better," Ten said.

"But you can eat them in one bite," Eleven said. "Besides, they're so hard to catch."

"I love robins," Twelve said. "They're very careless when they catch a worm."

While Lila and I listened in horror, the three of them argued about which bird tasted best.

"Ugh," Lila said. "I could never kill a bird or anything else. And I'd never eat one. That's gross beyond gross."

"Oh, fiddlesticks," Twelve said. "It might be hard at first, while you're still all girly girl, but you'll get over that soon enough."

"Not us," I said. "We'll run away like Thir—"

"Hush! Don't say her name," Ten cried. "It's forbidden."

Eleven said, "She-who-can't-be-named spent a lot of time in the dungeon before you rescued her, Fourteen. She was always in trouble, a very bad actor, that one."

"Mistress will make sure you two never escape," Twelve said. "You must be punished for stealing that cat, Fourteen."

"Aiding and abetting," Ten said.

"Mistress will get Thirteen back. No one escapes from her. She's all-powerful." Eleven's voice shook with awe as she spoke of Miss Dupree. "We worship her, we adore her. Without Mistress, we'd live in gutters and sewers and starve to death."

An old cat entered the room so silently, I hadn't known she was there until she spoke to me. "So, nasty little troublemaker, you're one of us now."

It was the cat who'd chased Nia out of my yard and later tried to claw through the window screen into Aunt Alice's house. I moved closer to Lila and watched the old cat stalk toward me.

"When you were a girl, bigger than you are now, you were scared of me," she said. "Tell me how much scarier it is to be smaller than me."

To hide my fear, I went all cat. I puffed up my tail and arched my back. I felt strong, powerful, unafraid. *Hiss, hiss, hiss!*

"Well, well, you learn fast," the leader snarled. Rearing up, she swatted me the way she'd swatted Nia. Down I went, no longer the proud cat. When she raised her paw again, I obeyed the instinct to lie on my back and surrender. I was too new at this game to fight with her.

"Too bad we got rid of one nasty cat only to get two more. It's like trading the pot for two kettles." She hissed and sprayed her foul breath in my face. "From now on, you and your friend better do everything I say. I'm Two, the boss here. Any sass from you and I tell Mistress. Got it?"

She turned away and joined the rest of her cronies on the

other side of the room. All nine of them stared at Lila and me. It was like being shot with arrows dipped in hate.

A one-eyed cat, the ugliest of them all, asked, "What did Mistress name the new ones?"

"The thief from next door is Fourteen," their leader told them. "The other is Fifteen. Don't ask me why Mistress wants them. They're bound to bring us trouble."

They left the room together, glancing over their shoulders to give us evil looks.

Lila and I crawled under a chair and snuggled against each other.

"If only we could tell our parents what's happened to us," Lila said. "They must be so worried."

"If we could escape while we're girls—"

"You heard what the nice cats said," Lila interrupted. "Number One watches us all night. We'd never get away."

I drooped beside her, truly sorry that she'd been caught. "You shouldn't have come looking for me."

"You're my friend, Zoey. I wanted to find you and tell you I was sorry we quarreled."

Like real cats, I licked her face and she licked mine. It comforted us both. Friends as girls, friends as cats. Together we'd find a way to break the spell and be girls again.

9

THE WHITE PERSIAN CAME SILENTLY into the room. At the sight of her, the cats, big and small, old and young, bowed their heads as if a queen had joined them.

"It is time for dinner and then the changing ceremony," she said. "Please come with me."

Lila and I immediately recognized Zleta's low, soft voice. It didn't surprise me to see her as a cat. She'd never seemed quite human — too sleek, too smooth, too quick. We'd never had a chance against her.

Crouched under the chair, we watched the other cats line up and follow Zleta out of the room. Lila growled. "I used to think she was awesome, but now I'd like to scratch her eyes out."

I didn't remind Lila that I'd warned her not to trust Zleta. I hadn't known her true nature then. And now here we were, trapped in cats' bodies, powerless against both Zleta and Miss Dupree.

A few moments later, Zleta pranced back into the room, waving her white tail like a banner. Miss Dupree was behind her.

"When Number One tells you to do something," Miss Dupree said to Lila and me, "do it at once!"

Lila ignored Miss Dupree and hissed at Zleta. "How could you do this to Zoey and me?" she asked. "I thought you were kind and beautiful. I trusted you."

Zleta licked her paw and dabbed her face. "I am beautiful—both as a cat and as a human. Unfortunately for you, I'm not kind. What cat is? Nor am I to be trusted by anyone except dear Aunt."

"You are my sweetheart." Miss Dupree stooped to stroke Zleta. "My absolutely dearest darling cat."

Zleta purred and rubbed her snowy sides against Miss Dupree's legs. She darted a sly glance at me. "If you'd given us Thirteen, you'd be home now. Such a foolish, stubborn girl you were. Perhaps you'll be nicer as a cat."

Miss Dupree looked down at us. "In the future," she said, "if you don't obey Number One and me, you will be sent to the dungeon without food. And there you will stay until I see fit to release you. Which may be never."

Zleta sneered. "Bow your heads to Aunt and me. Do not speak to us until we speak to you."

They waited for us to bow our heads. Lila looked at me, and I bowed my head. So did she. It hurt us both to obey, but we didn't want to go to the dungeon.

Meek as kittens, we followed Zleta and Miss Dupree. The kitchen was as bleak as the rest of the house—even worse because the sink was full of dirty dishes. Our paws stuck to the filthy floor, bulging garbage bags sat by the door, and the air stunk of cat pee and rotten food.

The other cats had gathered around a large bowl of dry cat food, the cheapest kind you can buy. The big ones crowded out the smaller ones, who ate what spilled out of the bowl.

In the dining room, which was painted black like everything else, I saw Zleta the cat seat herself on a chair with a red velvet cushion. Before her on the table was a china plate. From it, she daintily nibbled a piece of barely cooked salmon.

Even if we'd wanted to, we couldn't have gotten near the bowl of kibble without pushing past the other cats. I definitely wasn't eating from a bowl on the floor. If I couldn't sit at a table like Zleta and eat salmon, I'd starve. Lila turned up her nose at the kibble and groomed herself.

Miss Dupree finished her dinner and strode into the kitchen. Even though the cats were still eating, she snatched the bowl away.

"Follow me to the changing room."

This time, Lila and I got at the end of the line and did as we were told. What would happen next? Would we really be girls again, even if only for a night?

Miss Dupree led us to another large room with black walls, floor, and ceiling. Boards painted black covered the windows. She lit a candle on a tall stand. In its light, I saw a circle drawn on the floor. Evenly spaced around it were fourteen black dresses. Each one was numbered. Lila and I did what the others did and sat in front of the dresses with our numbers: 14 and 15.

Beside me was an empty space. A black dress numbered 13 lay there, waiting for Nia.

No, I thought, *she'll never wear that dress again. She's safe with Aunt Alice.*

Miss Dupree took a place in the middle of the circle and raised the candle over her head. Slowly she began to chant in a harsh language. The candle's flame wavered, sending shadows dancing across the walls and ceiling. Miss Dupree's long hair, free from its bun, hung loosely around her face. In the candle's light, she was both beautiful and menacing, her eyes deeply shadowed and her cheekbones sharp.

My heart beat faster at the thought of being myself again, if only until sunrise. I braced myself for the pain I'd felt after I became a cat. I sensed the same tension in Lila's body. I longed to reach out and grip her paw, but we weren't quite close enough to touch.

This time I scarcely realized the change was happening. My cat body flowed into my human body like water filling a bowl. In a few seconds, a circle of naked girls and women knelt on the floor. Watching the others, Lila and I staggered to our feet and pulled the dresses over our heads. They were no more than sacks of thin cloth with holes for our heads and arms, but they covered our bodies.

Lila and I turned to each other. She was there, my friend, just as she'd always looked. We threw our arms around each other and sobbed.

Zleta, now in human form, grabbed our hair and yanked us

apart. "No touching," she said. "No talking. Get in line and follow the others upstairs."

Lila and I took a place behind Seven, a pale woman with red hair, and Twelve, a skinny teenager with dark skin and curly hair. They climbed the creaky steps, their bare feet as soundless as a cat's paws.

Ten and Eleven followed Lila and me. Ten was now tall, tan, and blond, and Eleven was a small girl with tawny skin and black hair. They looked to be about the same age as Twelve, a little older than Lila and me.

Twelve looked over her shoulder at us. "Are you happy to be girls again?"

"Only if we get out of here," I said.

"And never be a cat again," Lila added. "Or be in this house or —"

Ten poked Lila in the back. "Hush. You'll get us all in trouble! We're not allowed to talk to you." She pointed a warning finger at a figure at the top of the stairs.

A woman with one eye and a scarred face sat there, looking down at us. I recognized her at once as the cat who'd asked our names. She frowned at Twelve. "Mistress has forbidden us to socialize with the criminals who stole the one whose name we do not say."

Twelve moved closer to the woman beside her, and Ten and Eleven ignored us as if they'd never spoken to us.

We followed the line upstairs and into a long brightly lit room. Ultra-modern sewing machines sat in rows on long tables.

Some of the older ones picked up neatly folded stacks of unfinished clothing and started to sew, their pale faces expressionless.

Twelve, Ten, and Eleven sat next to each other, but they never said a word or smiled. Somehow, even though they looked like girls, they had a sort of catness about them.

At one end of the room, a row of finished dresses in shades of beige, white, red, and black hung from clothing racks. Some were prints; others were solid colors. Like the clothing Miss Dupree wore, the dresses were made of soft, silky cloth. Mom would have loved their classic style. If she got the promotion she wanted, she might be able to afford these clothes.

Jackets and skirts made of heavier material, in the same colors as the dresses, hung nearby. Slacks and tunics and shirts, as well as scarves as light as silk, swayed in a breeze that slipped through the barred windows. Most of them were also black, white, beige, and red. No blues, though, no purples, greens, or yellows.

A few of the girls began folding finished clothing and packing it in tissue-lined boxes. Like the seamstresses, they said nothing to each other but worked quickly to fill box after box.

Nine, a pale teenager with a tired face, gave Lila and me pincushions, scissors, a bolt of fabric, and tissue-paper pattern pieces.

"Make sure you pin the pieces with the grain of the fabric. Like this." She picked up a pattern piece to show us what she meant. "Don't waste fabric. Cut carefully. The seamstresses need correctly cut pieces to do their work."

After watching us pin the tissue and cut the fabric, she left us on our own and returned to her pattern pieces. I glanced at Lila and made a face. It was easy, but boring.

Hours passed. The machines whirred. The sound made me unbearably sleepy. It was hard to believe that my bed was just next door. *If only I were there, not here, sound asleep with Nia beside me. If only, if only . . .*

A stinging slap woke me. "Don't you dare fall asleep, Fourteen. Three times and it's down to the dungeon," Zleta said. "Do you understand?"

"I'm not used to being up all night."

"You'd better get used to it fast. You won't like the dungeon."

She crossed the room and snatched the dress Number Twelve was sewing. She held it up and scowled. "Take this sleeve out and sew it in properly. Look at all those puckers. Do you think wealthy women will buy Miss Dupree's clothing if it's badly made?"

Twelve bowed her head. "I apologize. I was careless and clumsy."

Zleta threw the dress down. "This is your second warning, Twelve."

"Please forgive me. I'll do better, I promise."

Without acknowledging Twelve's apology, Zleta flounced off to find fault with someone else. "Look at this collar! Will you never learn to do it properly?" she hissed.

Lila and I kept our heads down and worked. Zleta sat in a comfortable black armchair and watched us, quick to jump up and pounce on anyone who made a mistake.

Her stare kept me awake, but my fingers were clumsy and slow. At any moment, she'd accuse me of wasting fabric.

When dawn's light finally crept into the room, the women and girls rose and tidied their work areas. We filed silently downstairs to the changing room and sat in our places. Following the example of the others, Lila and I took off our dresses and laid them neatly in front of us. As ugly and itchy as the dress was, I hated taking it off. It was like girls' showers in gym class—I detested undressing in front of other people.

Miss Dupree entered the room, lit the candle, and went through the ritual. A sharp jolt, and I was a cat again, a cat among cats. It was back to all fours to make our way to the kitchen.

This time, Lila and I were hungry enough to push between two of the others and grab our share of the kibble. The multicolored bits had the taste and texture of the health food cereal Mom loved. A little milk would have greatly improved it, but I managed to choke it down.

When we'd licked the bowl clean, the other cats crowded around the back door. Lila and I joined them, eager to be let outside, Miss Dupree opened the door, and the cats rushed through.

When Lila and I tried to follow them, Miss Dupree kicked us aside. "No outside for you."

Now it was just Lila and me—and the two witches. In hope they'd forget we were here, we tucked ourselves under the sofa and curled up to sleep the day away.

Just as I dozed off, Miss Dupree's voice woke both Lila and me. "Don't rush away, Zleta. We have serious matters to discuss."

The two of them sat on the sofa, giving us a view of Zleta's red high-heeled sandals and Miss Dupree's black ballet slippers.

"I told you that girl was trouble," Miss Dupree said. "One look at her the day she arrived, just one look, told me everything about her."

Zleta murmured, "Yes, I remember, Aunt. You knew at once. You're never mistaken."

"And then," Miss Dupree went on, "she had to go and gang up with the girl across the street, the one whose parents made such a stink about that dog. If he hadn't chased my cat, he'd be alive today."

Lila nudged me. "I knew it," she whispered.

Suddenly Zleta's body tensed and she leaned forward. "A car just stopped at Miss Fitzhugh's house."

The witches tiptoed to the hall. Turning to Zleta, Miss Dupree said, "It must be the police. I hadn't expected them so soon. Fitzhugh must have been very persuasive. After they finish next door, they'll canvass the neighborhood. They'll even come here. They won't give up until they find those brats."

Lila cuddled close and whispered, "The police will find us. We'll be saved."

"But, Lila, we're cats now. How will the police know who we really are?"

"Oh no." She hid her face in her paws, and I pressed closer to her.

Now that they'd left the room, it was harder to hear the witches. Lila and I crept out from under the sofa and crouched near the doorway. We had to know their plans.

Miss Dupree had begun to pace the floor. "Face it, Zleta. We've been here long enough. Maybe too long."

"But, Aunt, this house is perfect for our needs. We have space for the sewing machines. We're near the city and its stray girls. We have Caleb to ship the clothing to our distributors. Surely we can stay."

"When I want your opinion, Zleta, I'll ask for it." Miss Dupree's voice had an angry edge.

"Of course, Aunt. I just thought—"

"Listen to me. That Perkins woman will tell the police I poisoned her dog. Fitzhugh will harp on Thirteen and the arguments I had with the girl. Others will complain about my cats and the appearance of my house. They'll say I'm strange, unfriendly, weird, witchy. I scare their kids. The police will come back with more questions again and again. We'll have no peace. No privacy. Cops, reporters, they'll be here at all hours."

She took a deep breath. "Worst of all, at least for the time being, we've lost Thirteen. How will I stay in business without her? Who will design my clothing? Who will do the artwork?"

Lila and I looked at each other, astonished. "So that's why she wanted Nia back," I whispered. "That's why the cat was so special. Without Nia, she's out of business."

Lila purred in glee. "No more trips to Europe, no more fame for her or Zleta."

Miss Dupree glanced at the doorway, and Lila and I froze. Had she heard us?

But Zleta went on talking. "You're right, dear Aunt, of course you are," she murmured. "I apologize for my stupidity. I should know better than to question you."

Miss Dupree hissed like a cat. "Indeed, Zleta. Make sure you remember who's in charge. Do not question me again."

"Yes, Aunt. Of course not, Aunt. I never meant to offend."

"Now, call Caleb and have him drive you to the train station. Go the back way, don't be seen. Keep your appointment in the city. Show Mr. Winston my latest designs. Tell him I need to go away for a while, but I'll be in touch."

"I will, Aunt." Zleta paused a moment. "May I ask when we're leaving?"

"Tonight."

Zleta gasped. "So soon?"

"I hope you aren't questioning my judgment again, Zleta."

"No, no, of course not, Aunt. I was simply surprised."

"Perhaps you don't think I have the strength to do so much in one night. Is that it?"

"No, truly, Aunt, you are the most powerful person I have ever known."

"That's better. I assure you I'm as strong now as I was twenty years ago. Maybe stronger!" She paused as if she was thinking. "Tell Caleb we'll need his help tonight with the boxes of our clothing line. They must be mailed to our customers at once. Everything else will be left behind."

"*Everything?* Even our own clothes?" Zleta was obviously shocked. "What will I wear?"

"Stop questioning me, Zleta. When I say everything, I mean *everything*. We must travel light. None of what we have accumulated here is essential. We can replace it all just as we've done before." She drew herself up, one bony hand gripping the railing on the stairs. "Now make that phone call to Caleb!"

10

AFTER ZLETA LEFT, MISS DUPREE paced the hall again. "Those girls, those wicked girls," she muttered. "They must be punished."

Lila and I huddled together in fear. What more could she do to us?

Miss Dupree pressed her ear against the door and listened. Suddenly she drew back.

"They're coming," she whispered to herself. "But they won't get inside. I'll see to that."

Grabbing a cane, Miss Dupree leaned heavily upon it. Her body seemed to waver for a moment. In less than a second, she changed herself into a very old lady with a kind face and an unsteady walk.

The police knocked. Once, twice, three times. "Are you there, Miss Dupree?" a woman called.

Slowly she opened the door and peered out. "I'm so sorry, Officer. It takes a while to get to the door these days." She leaned on the cane and smiled. "How may I help you?"

A short, stocky woman stood on the porch, notebook in

hand. "Good morning. I'm Officer Jane Stuart. Are you Miss Eugenie Dupree?"

"Yes, I am. Is anything wrong?"

"We're interviewing people in your neighborhood about two missing girls, your neighbors Zoey Madison and Lila Perkins. They haven't been seen since yesterday afternoon. Did you see or hear anything unusual between three p.m. and six or seven p.m.? A car, a stranger, anything that might help us find Lila and Zoey?"

Miss Dupree gasped and pressed her hand to her heart. "Oh, this is terrible news, just terrible." Her voice shook. Her hand on the cane trembled. "I had no idea the girls were missing. I hope nothing bad has happened to them, young girls like that."

She peered at the policewoman. "To tell the truth, harsh as it may sound, I suspect they ran away. They're just the sort of rebellious girls to do that. Sassy, both of them. Full of ideas, easily bored. You know the type. Probably into drugs."

"Thanks, we'll look into that, but I must say I haven't heard anything to suggest they ran away." She paused to jot something down in a small notebook. "Miss Fitzhugh claims that you and her niece quarreled over a cat. Is that correct?"

"I don't know what Zoey told her aunt, but she stole a cat from me and refused to give it back. It was my favorite cat, my dearest one, the sweetest one of all. I can't sleep without her curled beside me. Such a comfort she was. Such a darling." She paused a second. "Perhaps you could ask Miss Fitzhugh to return my cat."

"I'm sorry, ma'am, but a cat is of far less importance than two missing girls." Officer Stuart sounded annoyed. "We need to find Zoey and Lila as quickly as possible. We have no time for missing cats."

"Yes, yes, of course, I understand. I thought if you knew how important the cat is to me . . ." Overcome with tears, Miss Dupree leaned heavily on her cane.

Officer Stuart's voice softened. "I'm truly sorry about your cat, Miss Dupree, but please tell me if you saw or heard anything out of the ordinary."

"Alas, I'm ashamed to admit I can't help you. You see, my hearing's bad and my vision's even worse. Getting old isn't easy, dear. You don't know now, but you'll find out soon enough."

Officer Stuart gave Miss Dupree a card. "Thank you. If you think of anything, please let us know."

As soon as Officer Stuart left, Miss Dupree tore the card into bits and watched them fall to the floor as we scuttled back to our hiding place.

Tossing her cane into the corner, she bent down and peered under the sofa. The kind-old-lady face was gone. "Come out from there, you sneaky, spying little brats!"

We pressed ourselves against the wall and hissed, but she stretched her long arms under the sofa and grabbed us by the napes of our necks. Her fingernails dug into our skin and gripped us tightly.

We struggled and squirmed, but she knew just how to hold us without even getting scratched.

"My, my," she muttered. "It hasn't taken you long to become cats. The way you've taken to your new lives, I suspect you're already forgetting what you were."

"Let us go!" we yowled. "Let us go, you old witch!"

Still gripping our necks, she gave us such a hard shaking my brain quivered like Jell-O.

"I am sick of looking at your ugly, deceitful faces. So much trouble you've caused me. I should put you in a sack of rocks and throw you into the lake."

"No, let us go, please let us go!"

"Ha!" She shook us even harder. "You meddled in my business. You stole my cat. Without Thirteen, my career is finished. I must move and begin all over again. At my age! You are to blame for it all!"

Despite our twists and hisses and yowls, Miss Dupree dug her sharp nails deeper into our necks. With one foot, she kicked open a door in the kitchen. Cold, stale air rushed up from the darkness, bringing with it the stink of decay and rot.

With Lila and me bouncing and swaying in her grasp, she ran down a flight of rickety steps, kicked another door open, and hurled us into the darkest darkness I'd ever seen. We landed on a hard floor with a thud. The door slammed shut, and a key turned in a lock.

"There, see how you like my dungeon!" Miss Dupree cried. "You'll die here and no one will ever know what happened to you!"

We heard her feet on the stairs. The door to the kitchen

slammed shut. We'd been captured like girls in the sort of fairy tale that always has a happy ending. But I sensed that this story, our story, the one we'd trapped ourselves in, would not end happily.

Lila and I crouched so close to each other, I couldn't tell where I ended and she started. In the darkness, unseen things slithered and scratched and squeaked.

A rat came near enough for me to smell its foul breath. I hissed at it, and it vanished into the darkness, squeaking to its companions. Their eyes gleamed in a glimmer of light from somewhere above us. I couldn't see well enough to count how many rats swarmed in the shadows, but it might have been a dozen or even more.

"Where are we?" I pawed at lumps of hard, dusty stuff on the floor. "What's this?"

"There's a big heap of it behind you." Lila went closer to it and sniffed. A few chunks came rattling down and bounced across the floor.

"It's a coal bin," she said. "My grandmother had one in her basement. They burned the coal in a furnace to heat the house." She looked up. "There should be a little door on the wall where a truck dumped in the coal."

"There it is," I said. "See? It's where the little ray of light comes in."

We stood on our hind legs and tried to climb the wall, but even our sharp claws couldn't get a grip on it. After three or four attempts, I had a better idea.

"I'll stand on your back," I told Lila, "like pyramids in gym class. The wood seems softer higher up. Rotten, maybe."

Lila braced herself and I jumped on her back. Struggling to keep my balance, I stood on my hind legs. This time, I managed to dig my claws into the wood. Despite slipping and falling more than once, I slowly climbed high enough to reach the little door, and then I fell. I tried again and again, but at last I lay on the floor, utterly exhausted.

"Get up. Let me try."

I had just enough strength to support her weight. She struggled, just as I had, but she finally collapsed on the floor beside me.

"We can't do it," she said.

"You heard what Miss Dupree said. Do you want to die here?"

"Just let me rest," Lila murmured. "Then we'll try again."

We needed more than rest. We were hungry and thirsty. Without food and water, we'd never have the strength to open that little door.

Hours passed. We took turns trying to reach the door, but no matter how close we got, we always fell back.

"Do you remember the story about the Greek guy and the stone?" Lila asked.

"Sisyphus, sure. Zeus made him push this stone to the top of a steep hill, but—"

"Every time he was almost there," Lila said, "the stone rolled down to the bottom of the hill, and he had to start over again."

"For all eternity," I said.

Lila sighed. "Maybe Miss Dupree punished us with the same curse."

We stared up at the door—so near, so far, our only way out.

"Oh, Zoey, I almost forgot! When night comes, maybe we'll change back to girls. We can push the door up and run home."

Of course. As girls, we'd have no problem escaping. Goodbye, Miss Dupree! Hello, Aunt Alice!

In the shadows, the rats chittered to each other. Chunks of coal slid down the pile and rolled across the floor. The rats were coming closer. We saw their eyes. We smelled their breath. Without thinking, we did what cats do—arched our backs and puffed our tails and hissed into the darkness.

Out of sight, the rats talked to each other in a harsh language of high-pitched squeaks. They'd attack again, but maybe by then, we'd have changed to girls and escaped.

We hunkered down, pressed close to each other, and waited for night to bring the change.

Just as I was dozing off to sleep, I heard a voice call my name.

"Don't answer," Lila whispered. "It's a trick."

The voice called again. "Zoey, it's me, Nia."

We'd never heard Nia do anything but meow, but now that Lila and I were cats, we understood every word.

"Get us out!" I shouted. "There must be a thousand rats down here."

Overhead, Nia tore at the door with her claws, but she couldn't pull it open. "It's been nailed shut!"

"Aunt Alice will know what to do. Can you make her follow you?"

"I'll be right back!" Nia dashed away.

"We're safe!" Lila cried. "Your aunt will get us out, and as soon as we're girls, we'll go to the police and tell them about Dupree!"

"Miss Dupree will go to jail! And all her cats will go to the pound!" I yelled. "Even Zleta!"

"Especially Zleta!"

Lila and I did a cat version of a high-five. The rats stirred in the coal but they didn't attack. They must have known we'd soon be gone.

A few minutes later, I heard Aunt Alice's voice. "All right, Nia, all right, I'm coming. What do you want to show me?"

Nia mewed loudly: "Hurry up! Hurry up!"

"Aunt Alice, Aunt Alice," I cried, "it's me, Zoey. Lila and I are trapped down here."

"Do I hear a cat?" Aunt Alice's voice was directly over our heads now.

"It's us," I yowled. "Hurry. There are rats everywhere!"

"The poor cat sounds so pitiful." Aunt Alice pulled and tugged at the door and swore a little. "It's nailed shut. I need a crowbar!"

We listened to her crash away through the bushes.

"Why doesn't she understand us?" Lila asked. "Miss Dupree did."

"Maybe only witches know cat talk," I said. "As soon as we change back to girls, everything will be okay."

Lila looked up at the crack in the door. "I hope it will be dark soon."

Aunt Alice came back then and went to work with her crowbar. After a struggle and a little more swearing, she pried the door open.

Almost blinded by bright sunlight, we squinted up at my aunt. She reached down, grabbed us by the napes of our necks, lifted us out of the coal bin, and set us on the ground.

"Aunt Alice, Aunt Alice!" I licked her hands and purred.

"I'm here too." Lila rubbed against my aunt's ankles.

"Such sweet cats. You must be so happy to be out of that place."

I sat up on my haunches and pawed at her jeans. "Soon we'll be girls again and you'll be the happy one!"

"Let's get out of here, kitties," Aunt Alice said. "We don't want Miss Dupree to catch us trespassing." She walked off without checking to see if we were following her.

We hurried after her. We certainly did not want to be caught trespassing. Miss Dupree would probably change Aunt Alice into a cat and put us all in a sack and throw us into the lake.

Nia caught up with Lila and me and we stopped to talk. "You saved me, Zoey, and now I've saved you!"

"Thank you, thank you, thank you." I rubbed my face against

hers. It was so odd to be a cat like her and not a girl. "I can understand you now, every single word!"

"Guess what," Lila said to Nia. "We found out why you're so special! You draw and design all Miss Dupree's fashions. Without you, she's nothing—she said so yourself."

"That's right." Oddly, Nia didn't look proud of herself. If anything, she seemed ashamed. "Dupree became rich and famous because of me. That's nothing to brag about."

"It wasn't your fault," I said. "She's a witch. She had power over you."

Nia hunched her shoulders and toyed with a beetle she found in the weeds. "Did you learn anything else?"

"She's leaving tonight," Lila said, "and taking everything with her."

Nia perked up. Giving the beetle a swat, she said, "I expected that. But not this soon. We need to keep an eye on her."

"When the sun sets, we'll be girls again," Lila said. "We can tell the police who she is and they'll put her in jail."

"Don't count on it, Lila."

"What's the matter?" Lila asked. "You look like something's wrong."

"I hate to tell you this," Nia said, "but you need to hear the truth. Only Dupree can change you back to girls. You must be sitting in the circle, with your black dresses folded neatly in front of you, and she must say the undoing spell. Otherwise—"

"Are you saying we might be cats forever?" I asked.

Nia bowed her head. "If Dupree doesn't break the spell, none of us will ever be girls again."

"But she's leaving town," I said. "How will we find her?"

"She's a witch," Lila cried. "How can we make her do anything?"

Lila and I stared at Nia. We'd been so sure we'd be girls tonight, but now it seemed we'd spend the rest of our lives as cats. We'd never speak to a human being again. Never do anything that required hands. Never ride a bike. Never go to school. The list of nevers rolled out into eternity.

Nia came closer and licked my face. "This is all my fault, Zoey. If I'd known Dupree would catch you, I wouldn't have dragged you into rescuing me. I'm so sorry, but being a cat isn't so bad, you know. I can help you get used to it."

"We don't want to get used to being cats." Lila glared at Nia. "The only way you can help us is to find a way to undo the spell."

Nia bowed her head. "I don't know how to do that, but maybe the three of us can come up with a plan."

Somewhere from the other side of the woods, Aunt Alice called, "Kitty, kitty, kitty. Come home. I have food for you."

11

IT WAS STRANGE TO RETURN to the house as a cat. Instead of opening the back door, we sat on the porch and meowed to come in.

Once we were inside, everything smelled right, but the windows were farther from the floor than I remembered, the table and the chairs were taller, and the ceiling was higher.

The colors were dull, as if they'd faded while we were gone. Red kitchen stools were gray. Green chairs were an odd shade of bluish greenish gray. Yellow walls were a dull grayish tan.

How had my aunt changed everything so fast?

Lila drew closer to me. "Nothing looks right. It's like being in a funhouse or something."

"Don't worry," Nia said. "You're looking through cat eyes now. You'll get used to the colors."

"I don't want to get used to them," Lila said. "They're ugly."

"You'll see better in the dark, and your noses and ears — you won't believe how much more you'll smell and hear."

Aunt Alice put three bowls of food on the floor. "You must be hungry, kitties."

Nia sat back and let Lila and me eat. We were so hungry we gobbled up her food as well as our own. It tasted better than Miss Dupree's kibble, but it wasn't as good as the human food we were used to.

While we ate, Aunt Alice brewed a pot of tea and poured two cups. Curious, I followed her upstairs to the guest room. She tapped on the closed door and opened it. I looked in and saw my mother. Why hadn't anyone told me she was here?

Before my aunt could stop me, I scooted past her. Completely forgetting I was a cat, I jumped on the bed where Mom was sleeping. Even with her eyes closed, she looked sad. A wad of used tissues lay beside her head.

"Mom," I cried, "wake up! It's me, Zoey."

She opened her eyes and stared at me in confusion. "Where did this cat come from?" she asked Aunt Alice.

Shocked, I backed away from Mom. Despite my fur, whiskers, and long tail, I'd expected her to know who I was. She was my mother, my flesh and blood—surely we had a bond a witch couldn't destroy.

I came closer and tried again. "Mom. Mom, I'm not a cat. I'm Zoey!"

She didn't pet me or even look at me but stared into space as if I weren't there, purring as loudly as I could.

"This is one of the two cats I rescued from a coal bin under Dupree's house," Aunt Alice told Mom. "They're both black like Nia. I guess they belonged to Miss Dupree, but they're just as sweet as they can be."

Mom looked at me with distaste. "I don't like black cats."

Aunt Alice set the cups down on a bedside table. "Do you want me to take her away so you can drink your tea?"

Mom pushed herself up against her pillows. "Just keep her off the bed."

Aunt Alice picked me up, but I struggled to go back to Mom. She couldn't mean what she'd said. She was my *mother*. If I tried hard enough, I'd make her recognize me.

Mom picked up her teacup just as I jumped back on the bed. The cup went flying, and tea spilled on the sheets, the pillow, and Mom.

I ran under the bed and pressed myself against a wall where Aunt Alice couldn't reach me. I was not leaving Mom. Even if she hated black cats, I'd make her change her mind.

Aunt Alice didn't even try to get me out. She was too busy cleaning up the mess I'd made. After she'd remade the bed and Mom had changed her clothes, they seemed to forget about me, so I stayed where I was and listened.

"If that cat belonged to Miss Dupree," Mom said, "why did you bring her here?"

"You wouldn't believe the fuss Nia made. Believe me, I didn't want to trespass on that woman's property or take her cats, but Nia was very insistent. Once I got them out of the coal bin, I left as quickly as possible and the cats followed me."

"Are you afraid of Miss Dupree?" Mom asked.

"Not exactly afraid," Aunt Alice said slowly, "but there's definitely something disturbing about her. The way she looks at me, her eyes . . ." She paused a moment. "I feel like she's hurt us in some terrible, unknown way."

"What do you mean? She's an old woman. How could she hurt us? How could anything hurt worse than losing Zoey?"

I watched Aunt Alice's feet move away from the window and to the bed as if she thought Miss Dupree was listening to every word she said.

"I'm not sure how you'll take this, Ellen, but Zoey was convinced Miss Dupree was a witch. Of course, I didn't believe her, but maybe I should have paid more attention—"

The bed creaked as if Mom had just sat up. "Zoey is missing, Alice. And you start talking about witches. It's unbelievable!" Mom's voice rose and she sounded close to tears.

"You haven't met Miss Dupree. The way she came after Zoey, the things she said to her, the threats she made. The child was terrified!" Aunt Alice took a deep breath. Her teacup clinked when she set it on the table. "Call me a fool, Ellen, but Miss Dupree frightens me now as much as she frightened Zoey. I just wish I'd taken the child's fears seriously. If I had, I might have done more to protect her."

"Fairy tales, witches. For heaven's sake, Alice, this is real life. The person who took my daughter isn't a witch. Zoey's gone, no one's seen her, and I can barely hold myself together." Mom burst into tears and the bed creaked as if she'd lain down again.

"Ellen, oh lord, please forgive me. I'm so sorry. I didn't mean to upset you."

Mom said nothing. Aunt Alice sat beside her for a while but finally gave up and left the room.

For the first time, Mom and I were alone together, but sadly I was the only one who knew that. I lay under the bed and listened to her cry herself to sleep. It was horrible to be this close to her and not be able to beg her to listen to her sister.

———

I must have fallen asleep under the bed—it was late in the afternoon now. Soon the shadows would darken and night would come, but it wouldn't change anything. Lila and I would still be cats.

I crawled out and stood on my hind legs by the bed. Mom was still asleep. I touched a few gray hairs scattered among the brown ones. Had they been there the last time I'd seen her? I didn't think so.

She sighed and moved in her sleep. "Zoey," she whispered. "Zoey."

I patted her face, purred in her ears, toyed with her hair. If only she'd open her eyes and see me, not a black cat but me—Zoey.

Nothing I did woke Mom, so I left the room silently and went downstairs to find Lila and Nia. Just as I reached the last step, the doorbell rang. I ran into the living room and dove under the sofa. Lila and Nia were already there. We huddled together, sure Miss Dupree had come to get us.

Aunt Alice went to the door.

"Don't open it, don't open it," we begged. "It's Miss Dupree — she's come for us."

Of course she didn't understand the danger. She flung the door open and there was Lila's mother. "Jan!" she cried. "Come in, come in."

"It's Mom!" Lila darted into the hall and threw herself at Mrs. Perkins, mewing pitifully. "Mom, Mom, it's me, it's Lila. Take me home, please take me home!"

"Oh my goodness." Lila's mother backed away so fast she tripped on the rug and almost fell.

"Cats are usually wary of strangers," Aunt Alice said, "but this one has fallen in love at first sight! You should be honored."

"No, no, please, take it away." Lila's mother gasped. "I'm deathly allergic to cats!"

Aunt Alice struggled to pick up Lila, who fought to stay with her mother. "Come here, be still!"

Lila wrapped her front paws around her mother's legs and held on tight. "Mom, don't leave. It's Lila! You can't be allergic to me. I'm not a real cat. I'm —"

Mrs. Perkins backed out the door, dragging Lila with her. "Get it off me," she begged. "I need my inhaler."

Aunt Alice finally yanked Lila away.

"We'll talk later," Mrs. Perkins wheezed. "No cats!"

"I'm so sorry, Jan," Aunt Alice called. "I totally forgot your allergies!" She closed the door and dropped Lila. "Just look at me. I'm covered with scratches. What got into you?"

Lila clawed at the door. "Let me out! I want to go home!

Please, please, please, I want my mother. I want my father. Open the door!"

Aunt Alice tried to pick her up, but Lila dug her claws into the wood and scratched so hard she gouged the paint. "Let me out!" she screeched. "Let me out!"

"No, no," Aunt Alice cried. "You're safe here. If Miss Dupree sees you—"

Lila wasn't listening. Twisting and turning, tail lashing, claws flashing, she screamed, "Let me go!"

Aunt Alice held her at arm's length. "I wish I knew what's upsetting you. You're a very angry cat."

"I'm not a *cat. I'm Lila Perkins!* That was my mother! I live across the street! Why can't you understand?" She raked her claws across my aunt's cheek.

"Ouch!" Aunt Alice dropped Lila.

At that moment, Mom came downstairs. "What's going on?"

"She scratched me!" Aunt Alice pointed to her face. "Look at this. She drew blood."

Mom frowned at Lila. "If she's that unhappy, open the door and let her go."

I threw myself at Lila. "Don't be crazy! Your mother's allergic to cats. She doesn't know who you are. She can't understand what you're saying. Do you want Miss Dupree to get you?"

Lila struggled, but when Nia helped me, she lay on her back for a moment and then ran under the sofa.

I followed her and licked her face. "I'm so sorry," I whispered. "That must have been terrible."

"I thought she wouldn't be allergic to me. You know, because I'm not a real cat, but she started wheezing like she does when a cat gets too close."

"But, Lila," Nia said, "we *are* real cats now. We smell like cats, we eat like cats, we purr like cats. People allergic to cats will be allergic to us."

"Is that supposed to make me feel better?"

"Well, it's the truth," Nia said.

Lila curled into the smallest ball possible and closed her eyes.

I left Lila with Nia and went in search of Mom and Aunt Alice. They were sitting at the kitchen table, drinking coffee and talking softly.

Their voices told me they'd made up after their quarrel over Miss Dupree. A big relief. I'd been worried Mom might get so mad she'd go back to Brooklyn. She'd done it before when she and Aunt Alice fought. They loved each other but that didn't mean they never argued. Mom relied on scientific evidence. Aunt Alice believed in imagination.

I wished Mom had been at least a little open to what Aunt Alice had said, but that was her nature. If we ever became girls again, she'd never believe what had happened to us.

12

THAT NIGHT, AFTER MY MOTHER and my aunt had both gone to bed, Nia paced back and forth on the kitchen windowsill, her ears pricked, her tail lashing.

"What's wrong?" I asked.

"Something's going on at Dupree's house. Can't you feel a kind of disturbance over there?"

Lila and I jumped on the sill and peered into the woods. I couldn't see or hear anything except the wind in the trees, but Nia was right: something was going on in the dark.

"What's happening?" I asked Nia.

"I don't know, but we need to find out." She examined the window screen and found a loose edge. I helped her pry a corner open, and she jumped out and landed on the porch with a soft thud. I followed her, but Lila hesitated.

"I'm not going near that house." Lila stared fearfully into the woods. "Can't I stay here and keep watch or something?"

"Watch what?" Nia asked. "The danger's at Dupree's house, not here."

"There, you just admitted it. There's *danger* at her house."

"Come on, Lila," I begged. "Three's a lucky number, you know that."

She looked at me and then at the dark woods, shaggy against the night sky. "Do you promise to stay beside me, Zoey?"

"Of course."

"You'd better." Lila jumped onto the porch and we headed toward the woods. Nia led us to a hole the other cats had dug under the fence.

Keeping low to the ground, we crept toward Miss Dupree's house. The night was full of shadows and sharp smells. An owl flew past us, close enough for me to smell its wildness. Somewhere a fox barked.

In the dark, I saw much more with my cat eyes than I'd ever seen as a girl—more than enough to find my way through brambles and briars and weeds. I smelled and heard more too. More than anything, I wanted to explore the night and all its secrets, but before I was free to do that, I had to find out what Miss Dupree was up to.

We hid in the house's shadow and watched and listened. I was scared and so was Lila, but Nia might have been waiting to catch a mouse. No fear, just excitement. Lights shone in the upstairs windows, but the sewing machines were silent.

"Hurry with that, Twelve," Miss Dupree shouted. "Get a move on, Eight. And you, Eleven, what are you doing, you clumsy girl? Be careful with that box. The dresses inside are worth thousands of dollars."

The girls whimpered and cried, but Miss Dupree continued to yell at them. I heard slaps and blows and curses from Zleta.

In back of the house, a man called, "Get the boxes in the cab. I don't have all night."

We followed his voice around the side of the building. An old black taxicab was parked at the bottom of the steps. Wearing their black dresses, Miss Dupree's servants carried garment boxes from the house to the cab. In their haste to avoid Zleta, they practically tripped over their own feet.

"Is that all of the boxes?" the man yelled. "If there's more, you'll have to leave them. There's no more room in the cab."

"This is the last load, Caleb," Miss Dupree called. Turning to her servants, she led them into the house.

"Why are they going inside?" I whispered to Nia. "I thought they were leaving."

"*She's* leaving," Nia said. "They aren't."

"What do you mean?"

"She doesn't need them anymore. She'll change them to cats and leave them here."

Lila gasped. "That's really mean."

Nia shrugged. "She's a mean person. Haven't you figured that out?"

I stared at Nia, horrified. "How do you know that's what she does?"

"While I was her prisoner, I listened, I watched, I learned. I know things even Zleta doesn't know."

"But where will they live?" I asked. "What will happen to them?"

"What does Dupree care? Cats can't tell anyone who they are," Nia said, "or what she's done to them."

"She won't leave Zleta," Lila said.

"Sure she will. Don't you see? She wants to start all over again. No reminders of the past."

"But Miss Dupree adores Zleta," I said.

"No, Zoey. Witches adore themselves. She doesn't give a hoot about Zleta." Through with talking, Nia sneaked up the steps and peered inside. "She's finishing up the chant. They'll come out soon."

The three of us slipped into the shadows and waited to see what happened next.

Caleb stood by the cab and watched the back door of the house. He looked like he wanted to get going. Looking at him with my sharp cat eyes, I decided he was the kind of guy who hung around coffee shops in Brooklyn. Skinny, shabby clothes. Kind of young but not in college. Not working either, Mom always said.

At last, a big black cat I'd never seen before ran down the steps. Lila and I pressed closer to each other, terrified of her wild and furious look. Where had she come from? Beside her was Zleta in the form of Number One, as white and perfectly groomed as always. The other cats followed them.

Nia lashed her tail. "The cat you're staring at is Dupree. The perfect disguise, right? Who'd think an alley cat was anything but an alley cat?"

The hateful cat leapt into the passenger seat. Zleta tried to follow her, but Caleb reached over and slammed the door in her face. With a turn of the key, he started the engine.

Zleta jumped on the cab's hood. "Let me in, Aunt, let me in!" she cried. "You can't intend to leave me here!"

She clawed at the windshield and meowed. The other cats crowded around her. Some scrambled to the cab's roof.

"Don't leave us!" they yowled. "What will we do without you? Who will feed us?"

Caleb stepped on the gas. Most of the cats fell off and ran behind the cab. Others clung to the roof and tried to keep their balance, but when Caleb picked up speed, they were thrown to the side of the road.

Zleta was the last to fall off. Like the others, she picked herself up and followed the cab.

I looked for Ten, Eleven, and Twelve, but I couldn't find them in the mob of black fur.

"Why are they following her?" Lila asked. "I'd run in the opposite direction."

Nia watched the last of the cats dash around a corner and vanish into the night. "They need her. They don't know how to take care of themselves."

"The only ones I'm not sorry for are Number Two and Zleta," Lila muttered. "It serves them right."

In the distance, the cats yowled, "Come back, come back!"

"Quick!" Nia ran up the back steps and into the house. "We've got something to do before it's too late."

With me close behind her and Lila lagging, Nia stopped in the kitchen. Her fur rose and she sniffed the floor.

I got a whiff of something too—acrid, nasty, bad. "What's that smell?"

Without answering, Nia followed the odor into the dark hall that led to the changing room.

"Ugh," Lila muttered. "It smells like the stuff Dad squirts on charcoal."

"Hurry," Nia called. "We don't have much time."

The circle was still drawn on the changing room floor, and the dresses lay in their places.

"Quick," Nia said. "Find your dresses. Don't you smell the kerosene? She's going to burn the house down."

Too scared to move or speak, Lila and I stared at Nia.

Nia swatted us both. "Get the dresses before it's too late!"

Lila gasped and pointed to the small blue flames dancing at the circle's outer edge. "It's already started."

The dresses lay in order of their numbers. I seized mine with my teeth and began dragging it away. On either side of me, Nia and Lila struggled with theirs. The flames were growing taller—and spreading toward our part of the circle.

By the time we reached the doorway, smoke choked us. The heat at our backs threatened to catch our tails on fire.

"Hurry," Nia cried. "Hurry!"

The fire chased us down the hall. Smoke made it hard to see, hard to breathe. In the kitchen, the flames came close enough to singe the dresses. When we ran out the kitchen door, sparks nibbled our fur.

Hauling the dresses behind us, we collapsed in the woods and lay in the bushes, gasping for fresh air. Behind us, flames exploded through the roof of the house.

By the time fire engines arrived, it was too late to save the house, but the men worked desperately to keep the flames from spreading. Police cars pulled into the driveway. An ambulance braked to a stop at the curb. Soon after that, the local news van showed up. Bright lights lit the street and the woods.

Neighbors ran outside, still dressed for bed, and gathered in the street. Mom and Aunt Alice were there and so were Lila's parents. I'd have given anything to be standing in the crowd, holding my mother's hand.

It was almost dawn before the fire was out. All that was left were jagged walls and the chimney. Near the house, the firemen had chopped down trees. Others stood like blackened skeletons, stripped of leaves and branches. The air stank of smoke and burned wood, along with other strange chemical smells.

Slowly the crowd broke up. Mom went home with Aunt Alice. They walked side by side, their heads bent. A few neighbors gathered around them and Lila's parents. They spoke in low voices. They hugged.

Fire engines, police cars, and ambulances drove away. The news van was the last to go.

Gripping our dresses with clenched teeth, we dragged them under the fence and into Aunt Alice's yard.

13

ALTHOUGH THE SKY HAD PALED to gray, light shone from the kitchen windows. Inside, Aunt Alice and Mom talked in low voices.

Lila dropped her dress and started toward the house, but Nia stopped her. "Where are you going? We have to hide our dresses."

Lila whirled around and hissed at Nia. "You've been bossing us around all night," she said. "I *hate* this dress. Why do I have to hide it? What do I need it for?"

Nia twitched her tail. "Without that dress, you'll never be a girl again."

Lila twitched her tail too. "How do *you* know so much?"

"Back off, Lila!" Nia arched her back and growled. "I lived with Dupree for a long time. When I tell you to do something, I'm not bossing you around. I'm trying to help you."

Lila looked at me as if she expected me to side with her. I hated to let her down, but without Nia's help, we'd be cats for the rest of our lives.

I rubbed against Lila's side. "Please do what Nia says. We can hide the dresses right there."

I pointed to a huge forsythia bush in the middle of the back-yard. "See how the branches hang down to the ground? There's a big space underneath them, almost like a cave. The dresses will be totally safe."

Lila ignored both Nia and me, but she hid her dress with ours under the bush.

By the time we'd finished, the sun was up. Aunt Alice heard us on the porch and opened the door "Well, well, look who's here—the raggle-taggle cats have come home for breakfast."

Mom looked at us with absolute indifference. She hadn't bothered to comb her hair and she wore the same baggy T-shirt and faded jeans she'd had on yesterday. Without makeup, she looked older and sadder. A different person altogether.

"No need to make a fuss over them, Alice. Cats can take care of themselves."

I was beginning to think Mom didn't like cats as much as I'd thought. I wondered who was taking care of Suki. Desperate for my mother's attention, I stood on my hind legs and rested my front paws on her lap. "Mom, Mom," I begged. "Can't you at least pet me?"

When she continued to ignore me, I slunk to my food bowl, almost too depressed to eat. Mom had become a stranger to me. Someday, when I was a girl—*if* I was ever a girl again—maybe she'd be herself again.

While the three of us ate, Aunt Alice and Mom continued a conversation we must have interrupted.

"As I was saying," Aunt Alice began, "I woke up around three a.m. and went downstairs to fix myself a nice warm glass of milk. I heard a car and looked out just in time to see the mysterious old cab pull out of Miss Dupree's driveway. I didn't actually see her, but I'm sure she was in the car."

She ran a hand through her hair. "It was the weirdest thing, Ellen. As the cab pulled away, the black cats, plus a white one I'd never seen before, ran after it yowling up a storm."

"Are you sure you didn't dream that?" Mom asked.

"I definitely saw those cats. Dupree must have abandoned them. Does it surprise you she'd do that?"

Mom shrugged. "You know her better than I do."

Aunt Alice finished her coffee and set down the cup. "I hate to remind you, Ellen, but WVTV is coming at nine to interview us. It's already past seven."

"Oh lord." Mom pushed away her cup. "We've already told the police everything we know. Why do we have to tell it all over again to a bunch of reporters?" She was close to tears.

Aunt Alice reached across the table to hold Mom's hands. "I understand how you feel, Ellen. I'm upset too, but TV coverage might help. You never know, someone watching the news might have seen something, heard something, and not known it was important."

"Nothing will help." Mom gave in and started crying. "Zoey's gone. My daughter, my only child. What if I never see her again? How will I get through the days and nights without her? I can't bear it. I can't go on like this. I should never have let her spend the summer with you!"

In her haste to leave the kitchen, Mom upset her coffee. It spread across the table and dripped on the floor.

Leaving Aunt Alice to clean up, Mom ran upstairs. I followed her only to have the bedroom door slammed in my face. I tried meowing, but when she didn't open the door, I went back to the kitchen.

I was shocked to find Aunt Alice in tears. She was the one who held things together, Mom's big sister. If both my mother and my aunt fell apart, what would become of us?

Aunt Alice saw me and lifted me into her lap. "Oh, what am I to do? I've tried so hard to stay strong for Ellen. I've tried to comfort her. I've tried to convince her Zoey will come home, but nothing I say gets through to her. It's killing me. I love my sister. I love Zoey like she's my own daughter. What will we do without her?"

Aunt Alice stroked me and kissed me and wet my fur with tears. "It's my fault Zoey's gone. I didn't take Dupree seriously. I didn't protect Zoey."

She hugged me so tightly I could hardly breathe, but I didn't try to escape. My mother might not need me, but my aunt did.

"And now that witch has done something to Zoey and Lila, magicked them away, and no one believes it. I told the police about her dislike for Zoey. I said she'd threatened her. I told them how frightened Zoey was. They said they'd look for Miss Dupree, but they don't really think she had anything to do with it, an old lady like her."

She sighed and blew her nose. "I didn't tell them she was a witch. They would never have believed that!"

Suddenly she relaxed her grip on me. "Oh lord, it's almost nine, and that news team will be here any minute." Aunt Alice blew her nose again and wiped her eyes.

She hugged me again. "Thank you, cat, for being such a comfort to me." She paused and looked at me. "I can't keep calling you 'cat.' You need a name. How about Jenny?"

"Why can't you call me Zoey? That's my real name, my true name, the name Mom gave me when I was born."

"Jenny it is." Aunt Alice cuddled me, and I purred. If it made her happy to call me Jenny, then, as she said, Jenny I was.

Lila came into the kitchen and jumped into my aunt's lap beside me. "And you," Aunt Alice said. "While I'm in the naming mood, I'll call you Missy. Do you like that?"

Lila looked annoyed. "Lila's my name. It's much nicer than Missy, but what's the use of telling you?"

Aunt Alice smiled at her as if Lila had just said she loved her new name. "Dear little Missy, feisty and sweet. I'm so glad Nia led me to that coal bin."

Lila loved compliments. She made herself comfortable and purred. "I guess Missy is better than no name," she whispered to me. "It's way better than Fifteen, that's for sure."

By the time the news van arrived, Mom had washed her face, combed her hair, and changed her clothes—still a T-shirt and jeans but ones that fit her better.

She took a seat on the sofa, crossed her arms over her chest, and stared at the floor. She'd gone so far inside herself that no one, not even me, was going to get a word out of her.

Lila's parents arrived to share the interview. Her mom clutched her inhaler and sank down on the sofa beside Mom. They said nothing, but held hands like sisters.

When Lila ran into the room and tried to climb into her mother's lap, her father told Aunt Alice to put the cats outside.

Out we went, just in time to see the news team arrive in a shiny white van and begin unloading their equipment.

Not knowing what else to do, we decided to investigate the ruins of Miss Dupree's house. We wanted to see what she'd left behind. Perhaps we'd find something to help us make the change.

Smoke hung heavy in the air. Ash coated the leaves and the ground. The only bird I saw was a crow, hopping from branch to branch in a charred tree. Croaking miserably to itself, it gave us a beady-eyed look and flew away.

Suddenly Nia turned her ears toward the ruins. "Listen," she hissed. "There's something there."

I heard a rustling sound and whirled around to look. "It's Zleta," I whispered. "There, by the chimney. See?"

Every hair on my body stood straight up with fear. Zleta— the two-faced monster, the liar, beautiful and wicked and cruel.

What was she doing here, so close to Aunt Alice's house? She wasn't finished with us yet. No way, not after what we'd done. She was here to hurt us.

"Quick," Lila whispered. "Let's get out of here before she sees us."

But Nia was already creeping toward Zleta, beckoning us to come with her.

Lila hung back, but when I followed Nia, she trailed behind me. Once we were near enough to see the cat up close, I thought I'd made a mistake. The newcomer looked nothing like Zleta. Her fur was matted and tangled and gray with dirt. Her head hung down, her tail dragged the ground. She limped as if her paws were sore.

"That's not Zleta," Lila whispered.

"It's her, all right," Nia said. "I'd know her anywhere. She doesn't have Dupree to wash her and comb her, that's all."

The cat moved slowly, her nose to the ground. Suddenly she opened her mouth and took a long, deep sniff. "You can't hide from me, Aunt," she croaked. "I know your tricks."

It was definitely Zleta, the two-faced liar.

Mumbling to herself, she turned away from the ruins and headed toward Benton Street.

"Come on," Nia said. "She'll lead us to Dupree!"

Lila hesitated, and I cuffed her lightly. "Don't argue. Just do what Nia says. We've got to find Dupree."

Lila hissed at me. "You didn't have to hit me."

From the edge of the woods, Nia beckoned to us. "Hurry up. She's getting away."

We slipped through the trees like panthers and followed Zleta down Benton Street, away from the library and toward the train station at the end of town.

At the railroad crossing, Zleta turned right on a narrow dirt road running along the tracks. We passed rows of ramshackle old houses, built so close to each other you could have shaken hands with your neighbor without leaving your front porch.

No Trespassing signs hung on fences, along with Beware of the Dog signs. Luckily the dogs were all sleeping in the shade and didn't even open an eye as we passed by.

After a couple of blocks, Zleta turned again and slowly climbed a long, steep hill. Where was she going? There were no houses, just empty lots overgrown with weeds and scraggly trees. The road dead-ended at a tall iron gate chained and locked with a rusty padlock. Beyond the gate was a wilderness of weeds and bushes and trees, but no sign of a driveway or even a path.

The white cat squeezed between the iron bars and limped slowly into the underbrush. Keeping a safe distance, we followed her.

At last we came to a mansion gone to ruin, just the sort of place Miss Dupree would call home. This time, the house she'd chosen was totally isolated. No neighbors to spy or trespass.

Zleta climbed the stone steps and scratched at the door.

No one opened it. She meowed and scratched harder. Nothing moved inside the house. Even the trees around us were silent.

"Looks like no one's there," Lila whispered. "Maybe we should leave before Zleta sees us." She was already edging away toward the gate.

Nia sniffed. "Dupree's inside. Smell her?"

To my surprise, I smelled her familiar musty scent. Such a thing would never have been possible when we were girls, but that tang of garlic and mold was definitely Dupree. Her essence, her evil self, floating in the air.

After a while, Zleta left the porch and walked silently toward the back of the house.

She stopped at a small basement window. Its plywood cover had been pried off, and glass lay in sharp pieces in the weeds.

Zleta stuck her head inside the window and sniffed. "Yes," she muttered. "Oh, yes. You left a trail you thought I couldn't follow, but my nose is sharper than you think. I've found you, Aunt."

She jumped through the window and landed with a thump, meowing loudly enough for us to hear her. We waited a few moments and peered into the darkness.

"I'm not going in there," Lila said. "It smells like the coal bin only worse. Much, much worse."

Nia sighed. From the slant of her ears, I knew she was annoyed with Lila. "Would you rather sit out here all by yourself and wait for Zoey and me?"

Lila didn't hesitate. "I'm so definitely not going into that basement—or any part of that house." She looked at me. "Please stay here, Zoey. You don't have to do everything she says."

"Please yourselves," Nia said. "I'll go alone if I have to."

Lila grabbed me with her front paws. "Don't go. You'll be killed. We'll never be girls again—please, Zoey, please! Let's go home."

I squirmed away from her. Nia waited at the window, ready to jump through. "Are you coming?"

I nuzzled Lila's face. "Come with us."

Lila pulled away. "Go ahead, get killed. See if I care."

I jumped through the window behind Nia. I heard Lila calling me to come back, but I couldn't—not now. Lila was perfectly safe where she was, but Nia might need help.

14

NIA AND I RAN through the basement as quickly and quietly as possible, dodging boxes and furniture and piles of stuff moldering away in the dark.

We found a narrow staircase that led to a narrow hall. Zleta was just ahead, her back to us. Slowly, hesitantly, she limped toward an open door. She was truly a pitiful sight.

"Aunt," she called. "It's me, your beloved Zleta. I've come to offer my deepest apologies for making you angry. I hope—"

"You!" Miss Dupree's voice rang out. "How dare you come here uninvited?"

She was so close my fur stood up. I cowered behind Nia, sure Miss Dupree was about to step into the hall and see us.

Zleta crawled on her belly into the room. "Please allow me to serve you as before. I will atone for my sins. I'll find another artist for you. I'll bring better girls to work for you. We can begin again here in this house, with no prying eyes to interfere."

We heard the rustle of clothing. Miss Dupree stepped into sight. She wore the same dress she'd worn when she locked Lila and me in the coal bin, but it needed mending and washing now.

"Just look at you—filthy, flea ridden, your coat matted and tangled with twigs and briar. I want nothing to do with you." Her voice cut through the air like a knife, sharp edged and dangerous.

"But, Aunt, if you bathe me and brush me—"

"Don't you understand, Zleta? I am *done* with you."

"Dearest Aunt, I've served you faithfully for many years, so many I cannot say their number. I've loved you and obeyed your every command. I've given you my loyalty. My heart. My soul. All I ask is a chance to serve you again, dear Aunt."

"What you did for me another will do just as well, perhaps even better."

"Oh, Aunt, please—"

"I'm tired of you. I'm tired of fashion. I have new plans that don't include you."

"You can't mean it. Without you, I am nothing."

"Yes, you are indeed nothing—nothing to me, nothing to anyone, nothing to the world."

Nia whispered, "How can she let Dupree talk to her like that? It's pathetic."

While Miss Dupree spoke, Zleta lay flat on the floor at her aunt's feet. "Have you no heart? No mercy?"

"You know I have neither heart nor mercy. Neither do you, for that matter."

"But I trusted you, Aunt."

And I was dumb enough to trust you, I thought.

"Witches can't be trusted any more than cats can." She

nudged Zleta with the pointed toe of her shoe. "Now go, before I send you away in the form of something far worse than a cat."

Turning her back on her once-beloved niece, Miss Dupree went into the room and let the door slam shut behind her.

Zleta stayed where she was. Not even her tail moved.

"She's finished," I whispered.

"Don't be so sure," Nia muttered.

When Zleta got to her feet, Nia and I edged back down the hall, taking care to make no noise, and crept down the basement steps.

The moment I crawled through the window, Lila ran to me. "How could you leave me here so long? I thought you must be dead."

I rubbed against Lila's furry side. "Everything's fine. Miss Dupree's here. She was horrible to Zleta, told her awful things and drove her away."

"Come on, you two, we have to go," Nia said, "before Zleta gets away from us."

From the gate, we saw the white cat at the bottom of the hill. She turned the corner, still limping, her head and tail hanging low.

We hurried after her, but when we came to the same corner, the sidewalk stretched ahead, totally empty except for a pair of mangy-looking black cats eating from a garbage can.

"Where did Zleta go?" I asked Nia.

She twitched her tail in annoyance. "Maybe she's hiding somewhere, licking her wounds."

"So how do we find her?" Lila asked.

"She'll go back to the ruins of the house," Nia said. "Where else can she go?"

Tired and hungry, we dragged ourselves up the hill toward Benton Street. The black cats saw us coming. They hissed as if to say this was *their* garbage.

Nia stopped. "I know those cats. Do you recognize them?"

"The ones rooting in the garbage?" I asked.

Lila looked at them with distaste. "They're stray cats. How would we know them?"

"It's Three and Five." Nia crossed the street. The cats stayed by the garbage can, watching her.

"Hello, Three. Hello, Five," Nia said. "I'm your old friend Thirteen. Have you forgotten me already?"

They narrowed their eyes and hissed. "We never saw you before," said Five. "What kind of trick are you playing?"

"They want our garbage," Three said. "We aren't sharing with you, if that's what you're hoping."

"Yeah, go find your own food."

Nia sat down and washed her face. Lila and I hovered behind her. She seemed pretty sure of herself, but Lila and I were scared. The cats looked wild. Half-crazy too. If they really were Three and Five, they'd already gone totally feral.

Nia persisted. "Come on. Look at me. We lived with Mistress for years. Don't you remember?"

The two of them growled and hunkered down like they were about to fight us for the garbage.

Nia scratched her side. "You can't have forgotten the spell Mistress cast on us. We were cats by day and girls by night. We sewed for her."

Suddenly Five stared at Nia. Her eyes widened. "I remember now. You're the one who ran away. It's your fault Mistress left us. I should kill you for that."

Five lunged at Nia, but the sight of Lila and me slowed her down. "One-on-one," she hissed. "Just you and me, Thirteen."

Nia lifted her paw. "I don't want to fight, Five. I'm looking for Number One. Did she run by here a few minutes ago?"

"That nasty white cat? Yeah, we saw her go by. She wanted some of our food but we chased her away. She isn't so high-and-mighty now."

"Did she go straight or turn a corner?"

"How do I know? She doesn't care about us, we don't care about her." Five glanced at Three. "Do we?"

"I don't know what you're talking about," Three said. "White cats, sewing, girls, Mistress. I swear, Five, you must be as crazy as Thirteen."

Three pounced on a piece of moldy cheese. "All I know is we slept under a car last night and this morning a man dropped a hamburger and I ate it and for a while I wasn't hungry but now I'm hungry again and I'm eating this cheese and I'm not sharing it with anybody, not even you, Five."

Five pulled a chicken bone out of the garbage can. "To tell the truth, Thirteen, I don't remember being a girl," she said. "In fact, I'm one hundred percent sure I've always been a cat. Mistress fed us and treated us nice as can be. We played all day and slept all night. Or maybe it was the other way around? Anyway, we had a good life, but like I said, you ruined everything getting into trouble and running away. So you can just pack up your crazy-town lies and get on out of here, all three of you."

Three stood up and added her bit. "And don't come creeping around our garbage asking for handouts, or we'll fight you to the death!"

"We don't want your garbage," Lila said. "Or your fleas. We have a home and good food and soft pillows to sleep on."

Three and Five hissed at Lila. Their tails lashed, and they started making that let's-have-a-fight yowl.

The three of us crossed to the other side of the street and kept walking.

"Three's completely forgotten her old life," Nia said, "and Five doesn't remember much of hers. If we're not careful, the same thing will happen to us."

"What do you mean?" Lila asked, instantly cross. "I haven't forgotten one thing about being a girl."

"Cats have short memories," Nia said. "If you stay a cat too long, you'll forget you were ever anything else. "

Nia looked back at Three and Five, who were now fighting over the chicken bone. "Dupree changed them back and forth, back and forth, from girls to cats and back again, hundreds of times," she said. "Long before you two arrived, the oldest ones had totally forgotten everything but their life with Dupree. In fact, Two thought forgetting was good, because you never miss what you don't remember."

I looked at Nia, suddenly scared. "You haven't forgotten your true life, though."

She paused and bit a claw the way people chew their fingernails. "I've been losing memories for a long time, more and more every day — my parents' faces, the house where we lived, the school I went to, my friends. I don't even remember my real name. Besides Thirteen, Nia is the only name I know. And you gave it to me, Zoey, not my parents."

"Ask me anything you like," Lila said. "My name is Lila Perkins. I live on Benton Street with my mom and dad, Jan and Frank Perkins. I go to Bexhill Middle School, I work at the library, and —"

Nia interrupted her. "You haven't been a cat long enough to lose your memory."

I felt sick. "Are you saying we'll forget everything?"

Nia looked miserable. "It starts so slowly you hardly notice — the title of a book, the words of a song, the name of a movie. But it speeds up. Every day you forget more, and finally, like Three, you don't remember any of your past."

I shook my head. "I love Hershey's dark chocolate bars. My favorite book is *The Once and Future King* —"

I would have gone on, but Nia stopped me. "Okay, Zoey, okay. I hope you both still know all that stuff next month."

Lila's tail twitched. "Next month? You're just trying to scare us so we'll do everything you say."

"Believe what you like, Lila. I'm tired of arguing with you." Nia turned her back and began the long walk uphill to Benton Street. Tired and unhappy, Lila and I trailed behind her.

"What happened to Nia?" Lila asked. "She was such a sweet cat when you rescued her. But now—bossy, bossy, bossy."

"Don't start that again, Lila."

"You're never on my side," Lila said. "Sometimes I think you like Nia better than me." With that she flounced off ahead of me, head and tail high.

I watched her go, but I didn't try to catch up. I was tired of arguing with her, and soon Lila was halfway up the hill and I was way behind both her and Nia.

Wasn't it just yesterday, or maybe the day before, that we'd been prisoners in Miss Dupree's house? We'd sewed all night for her; we'd been kicked around and half-starved; we'd been locked in a coal bin. Yet Three and Five had already forgotten the way life really was with Miss Dupree. They didn't remember they'd once been girls with names instead of numbers. Nia remembered Miss Dupree and Zleta and all they'd done, but she'd forgotten her girlhood. How long did Lila and I have before we forgot?

The yowls of fighting cats broke out somewhere behind me. Three black cats had attacked Three and Five. I was pretty sure the new ones had also belonged to Miss Dupree. Five had said she'd fight to the death for her garbage can. It looked like she'd meant it.

I couldn't imagine Lila and me fighting over garbage—but who could say what we'd do if we forgot our human selves?

We had to find someone to help us. Not my mother, not my aunt—I'd tried and failed to get through to them. Certainly not Miss Dupree—she'd left us to die in the coal bin.

That left Zleta. Impossible. Even if she said she'd help us, how could we trust her?

But Zleta's life had changed. She wasn't Miss Dupree's pet now. She had no home, no food, no water. She was tired, dirty, and hungry. She'd even begged Three and Five for some of their garbage.

In her heart of hearts, Zleta must hate Miss Dupree. Surely she wanted revenge as much as we did.

But how could we get Zleta to join up with us? And how could we be sure of her?

Nia and Lila were waiting for me at the top of the hill, just across the street from what was left of Miss Dupree's house.

"What took you so long?" Lila asked. "I thought you were right behind me."

"I was . . . um . . . thinking."

"You can't walk and think at the same time?"

"I guess not." Under my fur I felt myself blush, just like I would have when I was a girl. "I have this idea. You'll probably think it's dumb, but don't laugh, okay?"

I had their attention now. Taking a deep breath, I asked, "What if we got Zleta on our side?"

Lila looked at me in disbelief. "You're right, that's definitely the dumbest idea I've ever heard."

"Hold on, Lila," Nia said. "It's not such a bad idea. If—and it's a *big* if—but if we had Zleta on our side, we just might have a chance. I've seen Miss Dupree coaching her in simple magic, but it could be she's learned more than Miss Dupree realizes. Zleta watches things the way I do."

"Ha," Lila said. "I don't want anything to do with that cat. She'll double-cross us again if we give her the chance."

"You weren't in the house with us today, Lila. You didn't hear the terrible things Miss Dupree said to Zleta. She must hate that witch now."

"But how can we get near her safely?" Lila asked. "If she knows magic, she's even more dangerous."

"We'll bribe her with food," I said. "You heard Five. She begged for some of their garbage. She must be desperate to sink that low."

"It's a brilliant idea," Nia told me, "but we need to give it more thought. Like Lila says, we have to make sure Zleta can't hurt us."

For once, Lila didn't argue or complain about what Nia said. She looked pleased with herself for reminding us that Zleta was dangerous.

15

THAT NIGHT NIA, LILA, AND I sat at my bedroom window, staring out into the darkness. The moon was full and we could see the chimney of Miss Dupree's house poking up from the burned trees that once hid it.

Deep in the woods, Zleta cried, "Aunt, please don't leave me to die alone and afraid."

Lila swatted at a moth fluttering on the other side of the window screen. "She hasn't turned against Miss Dupree after all. What a stupid cat."

Zleta wailed again, closer this time.

Downstairs, Mom asked Aunt Alice what the noise was. "It sounds like a baby crying in the woods."

"It's just a cat," Aunt Alice told her. "Maybe it's trapped in the ruins of Dupree's house, like Jenny and Missy."

"It sounds human to me." Mom sounded worried. "What if it's Zoey?"

"No, Ellen. It's a cat in distress, that's all." A chair creaked as if Aunt Alice had gotten to her feet. "It needs help. Should we go look for it?"

"I'm not about to set foot in those woods in the dark. You could trip on something and sprain your ankle."

Zleta cried for Miss Dupree again.

"All right then," Aunt Alice said. "I'll get a flashlight and take a look for myself."

In a few moments, the beam of a flashlight played across the trees closest to the house. The light appeared and disappeared as Aunt Alice wove in and out between trees. "Here kitty, kitty, kitty," she called.

"Will Zleta hurt Aunt Alice?" I asked Nia.

"Don't worry," Nia said. "Your aunt won't find her. That cat knows how to hide."

The flashlight swung and Aunt Alice called, "Ellen, it's definitely a cat, not a baby."

Mom didn't answer, but Aunt Alice called again, as if Zleta was an ordinary cat. "Kitty, kitty, come here, kitty."

Branches snapped under my aunt's feet and bushes rustled. "Good cat, good cat. Sweet, dear, pretty darling. Where are you?"

We couldn't see what happened next, but Aunt Alice cried, "Don't you dare hiss at me, you wicked thing!"

Bushes swayed. The flashlight swung in arcs. "Scat!" Aunt Alice shouted. "Scat!"

The flashlight steadied and its beam pointed toward the house. A few minutes later, the back door opened and slammed shut.

"I've never seen a nastier cat," Aunt Alice told Mom. "I tried to help her and what did she do? Hissed and carried on as if she was going to attack me."

"You should call animal control," Mom said. "That cat is dangerous."

"First thing in the morning," Aunt Alice promised. "I should have listened to you instead of traipsing around the woods like a fool. See if I ever try to help that miserable creature again."

The three of us lingered at my bedroom window, breathing in the night. The air was lush with rich smells—damp earth and wet grass and growing things above and below the ground.

How had I lived for twelve years and not known how much a human nose misses?

"The moon is shining bright as day," Nia said. "Let's go out and play!"

Down the stairs we ran, out the kitchen window we jumped. The call of the night rang in our ears, our blood sang. We were cats. The night and all that hid in the dark belonged to us.

We ran across the lawn, jumped, pounced, and leapt in and out of the tall grass behind the garage. We searched the garden for the mice we smelled, our ears pricked for the sound of their tiny feet. I glimpsed a movement in the black-eyed Susans, but I wasn't fast enough. Lila saw a mouse and almost caught him.

Then Nia, long and sleek and glossy Nia, the panther among us, showed us how it was done. She caught the mouse easily and tossed it to me. I tossed it to Lila. We batted it back and forth; we pretended to let it go, only to catch it again. Chasing and pouncing, chasing and pouncing, we were players in a wild game without rules.

The last time Lila tossed the mouse, I caught it. My teeth grazed its neck and I tasted blood. Before I realized what I was doing, I bit off its head.

The body fell to the ground, and I spat out the head. In a frenzy, we hunted for more mice. I caught two, Lila caught three, and Nia caught five.

Nia poked one of the dead mice. "We can eat this, you know."

Lila sniffed the mouse. "Really?"

"Have you ever eaten one?" I asked Nia.

"Back in the days when we hunted together, Eight and Nine taught me to eat them."

Lila looked me in the eye. "I dare you to eat it, Zoey."

I crouched over the mouse, ready to sink my teeth in its body. But from somewhere in my head, a girl's voice whispered, *Stop. Humans don't eat mice. They don't bite their heads off, either.*

Suddenly ashamed, I backed away from the mouse. It looked so dead and so sad and so little all at the same time.

"Go on," Lila said. "Don't you want to do everything Nia does?"

"I'm not hungry."

"Hey." Nia gave Lila a cuff on the side of her head. "Eat it yourself."

Lila hissed and backed away. "*You* eat it."

We all stared at the dead mouse, its blood black in the moonlight. I felt like I'd murdered the poor thing.

"We should bury it," Lila said. "That's what I do when Dad catches one in a trap."

While Nia watched, Lila and I dug a hole, pushed the mouse in, and covered it with dirt. Lila bit a few daisies off and laid them on the grave. "Rest in peace, mouse."

Nia shook her head. "I never saw a cat bury a mouse before. Your girl voices must be pretty loud."

Lila took Nia's words as a compliment, but I wasn't sure that was how she meant them. Maybe she worried we weren't tough enough to deal with Miss Dupree and Zleta.

The moon was lower in the sky, not as bright as it had been. The shadows had lost their sharp edges. Deep in the woods, a barred owl screamed. We heard nothing from Zleta.

It was time to go inside. Lila and I ran up the porch steps. Before I jumped through the window, I looked back. Nia was still in the yard.

"Aren't you coming with us?" I called.

"I'll be in soon."

I looked at Nia, puzzled, and followed Lila inside. Before we left the kitchen window, Lila and I watched Nia creep across the grass like a long dark shadow, her belly close to the ground, her tail lashing, her eyes on the garden where the black-eyed Susans clustered.

"She's way more cat than girl," Lila whispered.

Nia disappeared into the garden. Flowers swayed to mark her path. It was true. Every day, Nia was becoming more of a cat and less of a girl. And so were Lila and I.

In the morning, Aunt Alice called animal control about Zleta. "She's a large gray cat, long-haired and very neglected. She might have been abandoned in the woods. Yes, that's grand. Thank you."

An hour later, a small blue van parked in front of Aunt Alice's house. A man and a woman got out. The man had a long pole with a sort of noose on the end, and the woman carried a no-harm trap.

We followed them into the woods, taking care not to be seen. None of us wanted to be caught in that cage.

The two of them walked slowly, looking for Zleta. "The cat could be anywhere," the woman said. "It's too hot to search the whole woods today. Let's set the trap and come back to check it later."

We watched them hide the trap in a thicket of small trees draped with honeysuckle and brambles. The woman baited it with a big scoop of kibble and adjusted the trap's door.

"That should do it," she said.

The two of them walked away, leaving a trail of kibble for Zleta.

All we had to do was wait for Zleta to wander into the trap. Time passed. We got tired of chasing beetles and butterflies. It was hot. We were hungry. We were tempted to eat the kibble scattered on the ground.

"Why not face it?" Lila asked. "She's not coming."

"She'll come," Nia said.

"I'm tired of waiting," Lila whined. "I'm bored and hungry."

Nia cuffed her. "Will you quit complaining?"

Lila backed away, ears flat, tail lashing, and hissed.

I wanted to cuff them both, but a sound in the woods stopped me. "Hush! I hear something."

Our ears swiveled this way and that, straining to hear. Leaves stirred in a breeze, and sunlight splashed down here and there, making shadows and dapples of light. Slowly Zleta limped into view. She gulped down some kibble, then moved forward and found some more. She was close enough now for us to hear her crunching the food.

She raised her head and smelled the food in the trap. With her belly brushing the ground, she crept toward it.

We held our breath. She poked her head into the trap, then crawled inside. Like magic, the door slammed down behind her.

She spun around and realized she was trapped. Screaming with rage, she hurled herself at the sides of the cage. "Let me out! Let me out!"

Her fury doubled and tripled when she saw us. "You! How dare you? Aunt will destroy all three of you."

"Not true," Nia said. "Dupree doesn't care what happens to you."

"She's on her way right now!"

Nia shook her head. "What's on its way is animal control. They set that trap just for you."

"Aunt Alice called them about you," I told her.

"She told them you might have rabies," Lila said. "There's only one way to find out. They cut off your head and examine your brain."

"They wouldn't dare!" Zleta said.

"Oh, yes, they would," Nia said. "To animal control, you're nothing but a dirty, bad-tempered stray cat. They'll put you down in a second."

Zleta narrowed her eyes and twitched her tail. "The very idea. Me have rabies? That's ridiculous." She was trying to hide it, but she was afraid now. I heard it in her voice.

"We can save your life," I said. "All you have to do is side with us against Dupree. After the way she's treated you, you must be really mad at her."

Zleta sat up straighter. "Why would I help you? You're nothing but common alley cats, but *I'm* a pedigreed Persian, Aunt's beloved companion."

Nia crept closer to the trap. "How much longer are you going lie to yourself about Dupree? We followed you to her house. We heard what she told you. She meant every word, Zleta."

Zleta crouched in the trap, lashing her tail against the sides. Her eyes glittered with rage. "Aunt *loves* me. She'll change her mind. She'll come for me, you'll see."

Nia looked at Zleta with pity. "She abandoned you as if you were no better than the other cats. What did *they* ever do for her? Not a thing. But you—you sacrificed your whole life for her. And look how she's repaid you. She called you ugly and disgusting. She said you were *nothing*. She told you never to come back. She even threatened to change you into something much worse than a cat."

"She was so mean to you," Lila said. "Don't you want to get even with her?"

I pressed my face against the bars. "Look at you, caught in a trap, dirty and full of fleas and starving to death. Do you want to live on the streets like Three and Five and eat from garbage cans? Wouldn't you rather be your true self and live your old life? You must miss wearing pretty clothes and all that."

"Side with us and we'll get you out of that trap," Nia said. "Together, we'll make Dupree sorry for every nasty thing she's done."

Zleta moved to the back of the cage. "I won't go against Aunt. No matter how she's treated me, I love and adore her."

Nia stretched her long, sleek body. "We're leaving now. It won't be long before they come to get the trap — and you."

"I'll never turn against Aunt," Zleta screamed after us. "She's just testing me. Now that I've proven she can trust me, she'll get me out of this trap and destroy you. She'll burn your houses to the ground with you in them!"

We left her screaming insults at us and headed for home.

"Maybe we should leave her in the trap and let animal control have her," Nia said. "No matter what we say, she stays loyal to Dupree. It's pitiful."

"She's afraid," I said. "Can't you tell? After a night in there, she might change her mind."

"Don't forget," Lila told Nia, "Zleta's our only hope. You said it yourself. Don't tell me you're giving up already."

Nia shot an angry look at Lila. "No, I'm not giving up. I've known Zleta for a long time and I'm sick of dealing with her, that's all." She paused to pounce on a beetle. "I wish I knew how much power Zleta has. Can she really help us? Or are we just wasting our time?"

Nia ate the beetle. It made a horrible crunching sound in her mouth. Not the sort of thing you like to watch — unless you're a cat through and through.

16

BEFORE WE VISITED ZLETA AGAIN, I used my clever paws and claws to pry open the door to the cabinet where Aunt Alice kept the cat food. I pulled out three packets of our favorite wet food, salmon in a so-called gourmet sauce. Nia, Lila, and I each carried one clenched in our teeth. It was really hard not to rip mine open and eat it myself, but bribing Zleta was more important than stuffing myself.

We found her hunched in a corner of the trap, apparently sleeping. She opened one eye slowly, saw us, and closed it again.

We laid the packets just outside the trap. "Look," Nia said. "We brought you food. Promise to help us and we'll give it to you."

Zleta hissed and turned her back on us.

"You must be hungry," Lila said.

She didn't answer.

Lila ran around the trap and looked closely at Zleta. "Are you sick?"

"Yes," Zleta whined. "I'm sick of you. I'm sick of Aunt. I'm sick of the world. I have nothing to live for."

"Remember," Nia said. "You don't have long before animal control comes—and then off with your head!"

Instead of answering, Zleta curled into a ball of misery and hid her face under her tail.

"I'm through with you! Stay in the trap. Let animal control kill you. I'm sick of this." Hissing in anger, Nia ran off into the woods.

"Stay here," I told Lila. "I'll be right back."

Before she had a chance to object, I left Lila and ran after Nia. She raced ahead like we were playing a game of tag, ducking under brambles and leaping over fallen trees. Sometimes she hid and pounced on me. Sometimes I hid and pounced on her. We forgot about Zleta and enjoyed being cats in the woods.

When we'd tired ourselves out, we found a sunny rock and stretched out on its mossy top.

"Don't give up on Zleta," I begged Nia. "You heard her say she was sick of Aunt. I think we can turn her soon."

"Mmmmm." Nia closed her eyes. "All right, I'll give her another chance, but I'm so, so, so sick and tired of her."

Bees buzzed in a patch of clover. Somewhere in the trees a mourning dove cooed. I closed my eyes and drifted into a dream in which Nia and I were hunting mice. We killed one, and she taught me how to eat to it without choking on its fur.

I woke up with an urge to hunt mice and eat them. It had been a real cat's dream, the kind that made Suki's legs twitch in her sleep like she was chasing something

I looked around for Lila, but I didn't see her. Then I remembered—I'd left her with Zleta.

I woke up Nia. "Lila's been alone with Zleta all the time we've been gone. Suppose Zleta has charmed her into being on her side? Lila's susceptible to stuff like that."

Nia stretched. "How long have we been asleep?"

"Who knows? Maybe an hour, maybe five minutes."

Nia jumped up. "Let's go."

When we were close enough to hear Zleta's voice, we used our cat skill to be as quiet as a breeze rustling the underbrush. Peering through loops of a wild grape vine, we saw Lila almost nose to nose with Zleta.

"It's too bad that Miss Dupree was so mean to you," Lila was saying, "but even if I wanted to, I can't open the trap."

"You could open it easily if I changed you back to a girl," Zleta said.

"You can do that?"

"I watched Aunt do it hundreds of times. I know exactly what to do."

"But how about Zoey? Can you change her too?"

"Ah, I might not have enough power to change her as well as you." She gave Lila a sly look. "But just think, if you were a girl, you could tell Zoey's mother where her daughter is. She'd have Zoey back—as a cat, of course, but that's better than thinking she's dead, isn't it?"

"I can't help you unless you promise to make Zoey a girl again."

"Sweetheart, all I can promise is to change you and then do my best to change Zoey." Zleta pressed her face against the bars. "Just think how happy your parents will be! And your friends! Summer's only half-gone — you'll have such fun when you are you again, my pretty, dear Lila. Think of the stories you can tell — the girl who was once a cat! Everyone will gather around you to hear what that was like! You'll be the most popular girl in school."

Zleta's voice was sweet as honey. If she'd been wearing her magical perfume, Lila would have been lost for sure.

Instead, Lila backed away. "I can't leave Zoey. You've got to change her too."

"Ah, but, Lila, you've forgotten your friend Nia," Zleta crooned. "If you become a girl, she can't boss you around. I know that cat so well — a troublemaker who thinks she knows everything. She's turned Zoey against you. That's the sort of cat she is. A liar, sly and deceitful. She has a plan for herself and Zoey. Why do you think they left you here while they sported about in the woods? Nia doesn't care about you. And neither does Zoey. You are a fool to care about her. Nia's her friend now, not you."

I whispered to Nia, "We'd better do something before Zleta poisons Lila's mind against us."

Nia put her paw on my head. "Wait."

Lila crouched by the trap. "You might know Nia," she said, "but I know Zoey. She'd never turn her back on me."

"Then where is she? Where has she gone with Nia?"

"I don't know, but she'll come back soon." Lila looked around like she hoped to see me.

"Pfft. You sound like me talking about Aunt. I've faced the fact that Aunt no longer wants me. You must do the same with Zoey. We'll stick together, you and me. *I'll* be your friend. Not Zoey. When we are once again our beautiful selves, we'll go to New York and launch your modeling career. Zoey and Nia will spend their lives scrounging food like Three and Five, but not you and me! We'll be brilliant! Glorious! The brightest stars in the universe!"

"But what about my mother and father? They won't let me go to New York with you."

"Don't worry, Lila. I'll make sure your parents don't interfere with my plans."

"But what if I want to stay here in Bexhill? What if I don't want to go to New York?"

Zleta's tail began to twitch. "I'm tired of your questions." The twitch got faster. Her tail thumped the sides of the trap. "Make up your mind or the deal is off!"

Lila edged away from Zleta. "I can't be your friend—I don't trust you."

"You're a fool, Lila. I offer you a great deal and you turn it down. You'll never be my kind of cat."

Lila looked around frantically. "Zoey," she called. "Where are you?"

I darted out of the underbrush and ran to Lila. "I'm so sorry! I didn't mean to be gone so long!"

She backed away and puffed her tail. "How could you leave me with Zleta? She kept trying to turn me against you. She wouldn't stop. She made my head hurt. I didn't know what was true and what was a lie." She glared at me. "What were you and Nia doing anyway? Why were you gone so long?"

"I fell asleep. We both did. When we woke up, Nia and I came right back."

Lila turned her head away. "Nia, Nia, Nia, it's always Nia."

"Please don't be mad. It's not always Nia—it's you and me and Nia against Miss Dupree."

Lila looked me in the eye. "Don't ever leave me like that again, Zoey. I mean it."

"I won't, I promise. You'll always be my best friend."

"Okay then. I'll be your best friend too."

We reared up on our hind legs and high-fived each other. "BFF!" Lila cried.

"BFF!" I echoed.

While Lila and I made up, Nia sat by the trap. "I heard every word you said to Lila. How can we trust you, Zleta?"

"It was a mistake. I was desperate. I wanted out of this trap. I can't stand it. I won't do it again."

Nia stretched and then washed her face slowly and carefully as if she was deliberately keeping Zleta waiting. "I don't know. Maybe we should leave you for animal control."

"No," Zleta cried. "I'll help you! I promise."

Nia tilted her head to the side. "You've changed your mind awfully fast."

"Listen to me," Zleta begged. "Last night while I was here alone in the cold, sad and hungry, it came to me that Aunt is truly done with me. I've seen her drive other cats away, but I never thought she'd turn on me. I'm angry now. I want revenge."

"But what can you do for us, Zleta? How can you help us?"

"Just think of all I know about Aunt, what I've learned from her, the skills she's taught me." Zleta sat back and looked at Nia. Her pale eyes glowed with secrets.

Zleta was in charge — or at least she thought so. She was telling Nia what she could do and Nia was listening.

"Aunt is old now," Zleta went on. "Much older than she appears to be. She's already begun to lose her power. I know her weaknesses. I can use them against her."

"Do you have any sort of plan, or is this just fancy talk?" Nia asked.

"Of course I have a plan. Do you think I'm an amateur?" Zleta lashed her tail. "First I change us all back to our true selves, and then . . ." She stopped to scratch a flea. "I'm not certain what happens next. I must be a human again to think out the details. My cat brain says pounce and kill, pounce and kill. To defeat Aunt, I must be more subtle than that."

"Don't make me laugh," Nia said. "We heard you tell Lila you don't have enough power to change anyone but you and her. Now you say you can change all of us and yourself too."

"I lied to Lila because I didn't want to change you or Zoey. I knew you'd never be on my side. But now, we'll be united by our hatred of Aunt. Us against her."

Nia tilted her head and looked at Lila and me. "Should we believe her?"

"You know her better than I do." Truthfully, I was still afraid of Zleta but I didn't want to say so in her hearing.

"I don't know," Lila said. "She's scary good at spinning lies, that's for sure."

"Let's go home and think about it," Nia said.

Zleta threw herself against the trap's bars. "No, don't leave me alone for another night. I see eyes in the dark. I hear growls and snorts, rustlings. I'm in danger here!"

"Nothing can get you in that trap." Nia pushed the packets of food into the cage. "You've earned these. We'll bring more tomorrow."

We left Zleta biting open the packets, too hungry to care if we stayed or left. The sun was setting and shadows had gathered between the trees. I pictured Zleta all alone, surrounded by the dark woods, cold and frightened. But instead of feeling sorry for her, I wondered what she was planning besides her own survival.

That evening, I sat on the floor beside Mom and watched her and Aunt Alice play Scrabble. It was the first time Mom had felt up to a game, and she wasn't doing very well. It was hard for her to concentrate. Aunt Alice made great words while Mom added endings to verbs. Stuff like that didn't add many points to her score.

I examined her tiles and saw a Z, one of the two most valuable letters, worth ten points. She must have been saving that *Z* for a word that would bump her score way up.

Well, *I* knew the perfect word.

I raised my head to see the other tiles better. Yes, she had an *O*. An *E* was already in use, but I didn't see a *Y*. Maybe Aunt Alice was holding on to that one.

Mom was too busy studying the board to notice me nudge *Z* onto the board and move *O* next to it. With great care, I removed *E* from *become* and slid it into place beside *O*.

Mom looked at the board. "The cat's messing with my tiles. See what she's done?"

Aunt Alice laughed. "Jenny wants to play too! What a smart cat!"

Mom put the tiles back where they belonged. "Now you know I have a Z."

I waited until she wasn't looking and pushed *Z*, *O*, and *E* back into place.

This time I was less careful and knocked several tiles off the board entirely. While I searched for a *Y*, Mom eased me away. "Go play with Nia and Missy, Jenny. Let Alice and me finish our game."

I hissed in annoyance, really upset that Mom couldn't figure out what I was doing. She'd looked right at *Z O E* and swept my name off the board. Then she'd pushed me away to punish me.

I reared up on my hind legs. I wanted to scratch her, bite her, make her understand. My ears flattened against my head. My tail whipped. I hissed louder.

Mom stared at me. "Don't hiss at me, Jenny. What's wrong with you."

"I'm not Jenny!" I yowled. *"I'm Zoey! Zoey! Zoey!* You didn't even notice the word I was making!"

Mom raised her hand as if she might cuff me. "Stop that! You look like a feral cat!"

"Why didn't you see my name?" Dropping to four legs, I ran upstairs to look for Nia and Lila.

Behind me, I heard Mom say, "That's why I don't like cats. They turn nasty in a second."

"Sometimes females act like that when they're in heat," Aunt Alice said.

"Maybe you should take her to the vet," Mom said. "You don't want a litter of feral kittens."

I found Nia and Lila and snuggled on the bed between them. Zleta had better turn us back into girls as soon as possible.

17

WHEN WE RETURNED THE NEXT MORNING, we found Zleta lying on her side, toying with a cricket that had wandered into the trap. When she saw us, she flattened it with her paw and ate it.

"Have you brought the food with the salmon and broth?" she asked. "I'm so hungry."

We showed her three more packets. "You don't get them until you tell us what you've decided," Nia said.

Zleta stretched and yawned. "Aunt has treated me abominably. She no longer deserves my fealty. I'll take your side against her. You have my word." She put her paw over her heart and stared at us without blinking.

"When will you change us?" I asked. "It has to be soon."

"When I feel stronger. Being in this trap has weakened me." She paused. "I've given you my word. Now release me and give me those packets."

We looked at each other. Until now, none of us had given a thought to freeing Zleta from the trap. How were we to open the door?

One of those idea bulbs lit my brain. I turned to Nia. "Remember when you brought Aunt Alice to the coal bin? Let's get her to open the trap!"

Off we ran, all three of us this time, leaving Zleta to eat her food. We found Aunt Alice in a rocking chair on the porch, reading the latest *New Yorker*. Mom rocked slowly in the swing, drinking coffee and staring into space.

Lila and I meowed loudly in Aunt Alice's face, and Nia knocked the magazine out of her lap. She tugged at my aunt's shorts and ran to the top step, where she stopped and looked back. She meowed too.

"Oh lord, what have you found now?" Aunt Alice asked Nia. Turning to Mom, she said, "Uh-oh. These rascals have found something for me to rescue. Do you want to go with us, Ellen?"

Mom yawned. "I don't have the energy to go anywhere."

"Oh, come on. A walk will do you good. They might have found another cat, a kitten perhaps. Or even a baby raccoon."

Mom slumped in the swing. "Tell me about it when you get back."

Aunt Alice turned to Nia. "'Lay on, Macduff.'"

The three of us ran down the steps and into the woods. Aunt Alice followed slowly, picking her way through vines and briars, doing her best to keep up without stepping in poison ivy.

At last we came to the trap. Zleta stood on her hind legs and peered at us, meowing as pitifully as a kitten in a pet store.

Aunt Alice saw her and gasped. "We caught that horrible

cat! I'll call animal control." She crouched down by the trap and reached into her pocket for her phone.

Nia jumped up and knocked the phone out of her hand, and Lila and I tugged at her shorts and her shirt. We meowed. Zleta continued to cry.

Aunt Alice stood up and looked down at her. "Poor thing," she said. "You're a lot less feisty now."

We gathered around my aunt, our tails high, and did our best to say, *Please rescue Zleta, please, please.*

Aunt Alice looked at Nia. "This is the same way you behaved when Jenny and Missy were trapped in the coal bin. I guess you want me to take her home with us."

We purred and rubbed against her legs. Zleta made herself look as sweet as possible.

"Once you're cleaned up," Aunt Alice told Zleta, "you'll be beautiful. You could use a good meal too. You're pitifully thin under that matted fur."

Aunt Alice squatted beside the trap again and examined the door's mechanism. "Yes, I think this is fairly simple." After a little fussing and fidgeting, she managed to open the door.

I expected Zleta to disappear into the woods, but she stayed where she was, as if she was too weak to move.

Aunt Alice reached into the trap and gently pulled Zleta into her arms. "My, my, look at these food packets. Who on earth has been feeding you?" She shook her head. "Another one of life's mysteries, I suppose."

I watched Zleta, still worried she might bite my aunt and

run, but she lay still and purred as if she'd waited all her life for someone to be nice to her.

Mom was still sitting on the porch, leafing through Aunt Alice's *New Yorker*. When she saw Zleta, she almost dropped the magazine. "Is that the cat you asked animal control to catch?"

"She was in their trap, but look at her now—the sweetest kitty you ever saw. Maybe she's learned a lesson." Aunt Alice stroked Zleta, who purred even louder. "How could I let them euthanize this sweetheart?"

We followed her and Mom into the house.

"Bringing that filthy cat inside is a big mistake," Mom said. "She's probably got fleas and worms. Maybe even ticks. You should take her straight to the vet."

"First things first." Aunt Alice put Zleta down, got a bowl, and went to the cabinet where the food was kept. She peered in and shook her head. "I don't understand where the cat food goes." She looked at Mom. "Are you feeding the cats extra meals, Ellen?"

"Of course not. You feed them more than enough."

Aunt Alice shifted her eyes to us. "Hmmm. I wonder if you've figured out how to open the cabinet. You rascals are smart enough." She looked at us more closely. "And you're definitely a little round."

We looked as innocent as cats can look.

Aunt Alice shrugged. "No matter. I'm going to the store tomorrow."

After Zleta ate, she drank a bowl of water. Next she bit and clawed at the mats in her fur. She tried to pull out twigs and brambles, but in the end she didn't look much better.

"What she needs is a bath and a good combing," Aunt Alice said.

"I doubt she'll let you do that," Mom said. "Even the sweetest cat in the world hates to be washed."

Zleta rubbed against Aunt Alice's legs and purred, pausing only to claw at the mats in her fur.

Aunt Alice leaned down and looked Zleta in the eye. "Do you want a bath?" It's the sort of question adults ask pets and babies: *Are you hungry? Do you want to go for a walk? Are you ready for a nap?* They don't expect an answer.

Zleta mewed pitifully and stood on her hind legs to peer into Aunt Alice's face.

"I swear, a bath is exactly what she wants," my aunt said. "Sometimes I think cats understand more than we think they do."

Mom smiled in a sad sort of way. "When Zoey asked Suki if she was hungry, the cat would run to the kitchen and sit beside her bowl. I don't know if she actually knew the word *hungry* or just understood Zoey's tone of voice."

Suki, Suki. That name was so familiar. Did I once have a cat named Suki? If so, why couldn't I remember the color of her fur? And while I was thinking about that sort of thing, was our apartment in Brooklyn on the third or the fourth floor? What did I see when I looked out my bedroom window?

To turn off the questions without answers, I followed Aunt Alice to the basement and watched her fill the utility tub with warm, soapy water. Zleta perched on the washing machine and waited for her bath.

Aunt Alice pulled on a bright yellow pair of rubber work gloves and tied a barbecue apron around her waist.

"I suppose you'll fight me tooth and claw," she said to Zleta. But when she dipped the cat into the water, Zleta purred and allowed my aunt to scrub her thoroughly.

Her wet fur slowly changed from dingy gray to a white so transparent that her pink skin showed through. Her tail was limp and scraggly. She looked like a large wet rat instead of a cat.

After the bath, Aunt Alice dried Zleta with a soft towel and went to work on the mats and tangles in her coat. Although it made me wince to watch the comb pull brambles, twigs, and beggar's lice from her fur, Zleta never even growled. The worst tangles had to be cut out with nail scissors, but Aunt Alice assured Zleta the missing fur wouldn't be noticeable. "Not with your thick coat."

When my aunt was finally finished, Zleta looked like herself. Which wasn't reassuring. Dirty and hungry, she'd been far less threatening. Now I saw her as she'd been in Miss Dupree's house—cruel and proud and as wicked as her mistress.

Aunt Alice had never seen Zleta as she was then. She smiled at the Persian cat now sitting in her lap purring as loudly as an idling bus.

"Oh, Queenie, you're much too beautiful to go to the pound," Aunt Alice whispered.

Zleta glanced at me as if to say, *See how good I am at fooling people?*

———

Sometime in the late afternoon, animal control knocked on the door. "We checked the trap," the woman told Aunt Alice, "but someone sprung it and set the cat free."

"Maybe the cat's owner found her and took her home," Aunt Alice said.

The man nodded. "That's what we think, ma'am. She'd even been fed." He paused to adjust the brim on his cap. "It didn't make sense to reset the trap, so we put it in the van. If you see the cat again, give us a ring. We'll bring the trap back."

"Will do," Aunt Alice said. "Thanks for coming."

"No problem."

She watched them get into the van and drive away. "It wasn't a lie," she told Mom. "We're Queenie's owners now."

———

Late that night, Zleta took us to a place in the ruins that she claimed was the old changing room. "The magic level is still high here," she said, "from all the transformations from girl to cat and back again."

"Will we need our dresses?" I asked.

"Those old rags? They were just something for you to wear when you changed. Aunt didn't want a room full of naked girls."

But, I wondered, wouldn't we need clothes this time? Then again, wasn't being naked in the woods a small price to pay for changing from cat to girl? After all, I had plenty of clothes in my aunt's house.

"How about the candle and the circle?" Lila asked.

"Meaningless, only trappings to impress you."

Zleta paused and glanced around the space she'd chosen. What was once a dark, closed-in room was now a roofless space open to the night sky and lit by the moon. Zleta's fur glowed in its light. Trees cast ever-changing shadow shapes across the dirt floor. Deep in the woods, the scream of a barred owl sent shivers down my spine.

Zleta looked at us. Her green eyes gleamed with excitement. "At last, a chance to show off *my* magic!" She clasped her paws over her head as if she'd won a great contest. "Sit down and do not move," she told us. "Give me all your attention. Do not be distracted. Above all, believe you will soon be girls."

We did as we were told. With my eyes fixed on Zleta, I chanted silently, *I will be a girl, I will be a girl.*

Zleta rose on her haunches, her front paws raised, her head thrown back, and began speaking in Miss Dupree's strange language. Her voice rose and fell.

I will be a girl, I will be a girl . . . My heart pounded as I waited for the change.

Zleta chanted faster and louder. The barred owl screamed, closer this time. Wind blew through the trees. Leaves spun

169

around us. Nia, Lila, and I huddled together, too scared to concentrate on changing.

Zleta stopped chanting and lay flat on her belly, as frightened
as we were.

The wind dropped, and the owl flew so low over us that its
wings brushed my fur. With one last scream, it vanished into the
night.

18

NIA CROUCHED beside the trembling white cat. "You lied again," she hissed at Zleta. "I should rip your heart out!"

"No, no," Zleta cried. "I wasn't lying. I was sure I could do it. I watched Aunt so often, it looked easy. I said the right words, but—"

"But it didn't work!" Nia cuffed Zleta, who edged away from her.

"I'm sorry," she said in a low voice. "From deep in my heart, I apologize."

I was pretty sure that Zleta had never apologized to anyone except Miss Dupree. In her previous life, she'd had nothing to feel sorry for. Whether or not she meant what she said now, it was impossible to know.

"Sorry? You?" Nia growled. "You have no heart, you said so yourself."

"What if I return to Aunt and ask her to take me back?"

"What good will that do us?"

"You know how skilled I am at spinning lies," Zleta said. "I'll convince her I've won your trust and friendship, that you are now under my power and will do anything I ask you. With my help, you will be her servants again."

"But we're not under your power," Nia said, "and never will be."

"All I ask is that you pretend to be under my power."

"I don't like your plan," I told her. "If Miss Dupree is involved, anything can happen. You might switch sides. We might be taken to her new house and forced to sew again, all night, every night, forever."

"I'd rather stay a cat than take a chance with Miss Dupree," Lila said.

Zleta turned to Nia. "You haven't said anything."

"I say we take a chance. Talk to Dupree. We'll go with you to hear what you say. That way, you can't double-cross us."

Zleta looked alarmed. "She mustn't see you."

"Don't worry," Nia said. "We know how to hide in shadows and make no sound. It's what cats do."

"When shall we visit Aunt?" Zleta asked.

"Now," Nia said. "Before it's too late."

If Zleta was surprised, she didn't show it. We left the ruins and headed down Benton Street.

The empty road and its dark houses ran down the hill ahead of us. The only light came from a street lamp on the corner. Every now and then a dog ran to a fence and barked. There was no other sound. In their beds, people slept undisturbed. They had no idea what went on in their streets late at night.

Nia, Lila, and I stayed in the shadows, but Zleta strode along the moonlit streets as if she wanted to be seen and admired. She held her tail high. It swayed like a plume as Zleta pranced, brilliant white in the moonlight, dull gray in the shadows.

When we came to the top of the hill, the mansion loomed tall against the night sky, dark and forbidding. We let Zleta lead the way to the basement window. She crawled through and we followed her one at a time, Nia first and Lila last. Nothing had changed since our previous visit. We made our way to the stairs, just as we'd done before.

On the top step we paused to listen. Not a sound. The house seemed as vacant as it looked from the outside.

"Don't worry," Zleta whispered. "She's here. I smell her. Don't you?"

We sniffed and yes, we smelled Miss Dupree's peculiar odor of earth and garlic with a little mold mixed in. Not a terrible smell but not a pleasant one, either. If someone offered me a bowl of soup that smelled like that, I wouldn't have eaten it.

Zleta twitched her tail. Even in the dim light, her eyes gleamed. "I hope to catch her by surprise."

"But she's a witch," Nia said. "Won't she sense we're here?"

"She's old, I tell you," Zleta said scornfully. "When you become a witch, you receive a certain amount of power. The more you use, the more you lose. It's like taking money out of the bank but never putting any in."

Zleta's tail had taken on a life of its own. The more she talked, the faster it twitched. "Aunt would never admit it," she went on, "but day by day, I've seen her power weaken. For example—that scene in the street with you, Zoey. In her youth, she'd have taken Thirteen and destroyed you. She also used a lot of her power when she left her house on Benton Street and burned it. She's hiding here in hope of restoring herself, but once her power's gone, it's gone. She can't get it back. That's why I will defeat her."

She gave us a sly look. "It's what I've been waiting for ever since she took me in. As much as I loved her, my secret heart told me she'd betray me someday. So I was ready." She lashed her tail. "I never expected it to happen so soon."

Nosing the basement door open, she peered into the hall. A dim light shone from a doorway near the front of the house.

"She's there, where she was before," Zleta whispered. "Now we shall see if Aunt is as weak as I believe her to be."

We started to follow her, but she stopped us. "Wait here. You three are not nearly as silent as I am."

We hung back and watched her creep toward the doorway and enter the room.

Nia nudged me forward. "Go closer so you see and hear what happens between them. I'll wait here with Lila."

"Me?"

"You. Be quick, be silent."

I slunk to the doorway. The room was poorly lit by a single candle, but with my cat eyes, I saw Miss Dupree clearly. She leaned on a cane, her back hunched like an old woman's. Her dress hung on her as if she'd shrunk, and her hair dangled in strings around her face. Unless it was a disguise, Miss Dupree had definitely weakened since the last time I'd seen her in this very room.

"Why are you here? I told you never to return." Miss Dupree hobbled toward Zleta as if she meant to hit her with her cane.

At Miss Dupree's feet, Zleta rolled over on her back, her dainty white paws in the air. "Oh, Aunt, dear Aunt, I surrender to you. Please be merciful. I come with good news."

"What good news can you possibly have for me?"

"You may be pleased to hear I have befriended Thirteen, Fourteen, and Fifteen. As well as Fourteen's aunt and her mother."

"That's not possible. Fourteen and Fifteen died in the fire. I locked them in the coal bin myself. They couldn't have escaped."

Zleta smirked. "Have you forgotten Thirteen? She led the aunt to the coal bin. Fourteen and Fifteen were safe before you even left the house."

"Thirteen again! I should have drowned her when she was a kitten." Miss Dupree paced back and forth. "I find it hard to believe any of them would have befriended you. They despise you!"

"Ah, but they despise you even more than me."

The witch stopped pacing and looked at Zleta. "Tell me how you won their friendship. I'm curious."

Zleta bowed her head. "I agreed to help them break your spell and return them to their former selves. Of course, I lied. My only wish is to help you avenge yourself on the cats who betrayed you."

"After all we did to them, they were stupid enough to trust you?"

"Modesty aside, I'm very skilled at the deception game."

"Yes, you're good, but don't forget who taught you how to play it." Miss Dupree turned away from Zleta and began to pace the room again, leaning heavily on her cane.

While the witch paced, I watched Zleta. She'd convinced us she was *our* friend, but now she'd convinced Miss Dupree she was *her* friend. Whose side was she really on?

Miss Dupree finally stopped pacing and frowned down at Zleta. "Indeed, you are so good at the game, I find myself wondering if I can trust you. To bring the girls to you, to win their trust—I don't believe you have the power to do that, Number One."

Zleta rubbed against Miss Dupree's legs and purred. "It stabs me in my heart to hear you say such things. When have I ever been disloyal to you? Why do you doubt me? You, my teacher, my beloved aunt, what I tell you is true. Human beings are foolish. They believe what they want to believe, see what they want to see. They don't look into the darkness like we do. They don't know what evil lurks there. They are trustful and easy to deceive."

Miss Dupree studied Zleta, who crouched at her feet, the picture of humility. "You were a filthy mess when I chased you away. Who cleaned you up?"

"Aunt Alice. She thinks I'm a sweet and beautiful cat. She adores me. What a fool she is."

My tail lashed. How dare she make fun of my aunt?

Zleta rubbed against Miss Dupree's bare, skinny legs. "I wanted you to see me at my best, not as I was the last time I visited — a pitiful creature begging you to take me back. No, I have come to you this time as one who can give you your enemies to torment as you wish."

"I don't need your help. You may think I've weakened, but I still have my strength. Be careful not to offend me. When I have rested a few more days, I will go forth and punish those girls myself."

"Nothing, not even the setbacks you've suffered, can weaken a witch as strong as you. You'll strike down your enemies and avenge yourself with or without me. All I wish is to assist you as I have done many times before."

"That's my Number One, my dearest Zleta." She sank into her chair and Zleta leapt into her lap. "You're still my precious one, my lovely Zleta, my star pupil. If you deliver them to me, everything will be as before. Thirteen will design my clothing, Fourteen and Fifteen will be my seamstresses, and you, my darling, will provide me with a new supply of workers. Of course, you will once again represent me in the fashion industry. We'll see Paris and Rome again soon, my dear Zleta."

She set Zleta down and clapped her hands. "Now, go, work out the plan. I must resume my career as soon as possible. We don't want the fashion world to forget Madame Eugenie."

"I'm sure you've been sorely missed by the many who buy your fashions. I'm eager to present a portfolio of your latest designs." Zleta cuddled closer to Miss Dupree and purred louder.

"Before I set my plan into action, I have one request. I hope you'll grant it."

"What is it, dear one?"

Zleta hesitated. "I need my hands to bind the cats. You cannot imagine how difficult it is to work with my paws. If you allow me to return to my human form, I can trap them quickly and easily."

I froze. As a human, Zleta would definitely be more of a danger to us. What if she was telling the truth to Miss Dupree and lying to us? How could we ever be sure?

Miss Dupree began pacing again. Each time she passed the candle, her shadow grew and followed her across the ceiling. As she walked away, it shrank. I watched, almost mesmerized by the shadow's changing size.

"You ask a great deal, Zleta."

"I beg your forgiveness for the audacity of my request, but with your great and ever-increasing power, it should be no problem."

"It's an issue of trust, not power. In human form, you're more dangerous to me. Swear the darkest oath of witchcraft to prove your loyalty."

"Gladly."

Miss Dupree lifted Zleta and held her eye-to-eye. In the harsh language I didn't understand, she spoke to her. Zleta repeated the words.

Miss Dupree put Zleta down. Kicking a rug aside, she revealed a small, elaborate circle painted on the floor. "Take your place."

Zleta sat still, as regal as the queen of the cats, while Miss Dupree rummaged in a closet.

Laying a shabby black skirt and T-shirt in front of Zleta, she said, "It's not the style you're used to, but it's all I have."

With Zleta at her feet, the witch raised her arms. The shadow witch did the same, except her arms wavered across the ceiling. She began to chant. Her voice, weaker than I remembered, rose and fell.

In a moment, the white cat was gone and Zleta the beautiful was pulling on her clothing.

"Now, be on your way," Miss Dupree said. "I'll meet you at the ruins of my former home tomorrow night at eleven."

"Be careful," Zleta said. "If anyone sees you, if you're recognized—"

"Don't worry," Miss Dupree said. "I'll come as a black cat. No one notices a cat passing by in the dark. Especially a black one."

While Zleta and Miss Dupree said their goodbyes, I crept back to the basement door and ran down the steps with my friends.

———

Zleta waited for us by the gate. Even barefoot and wearing drab clothing, she looked like the queen of the night. We followed her down the hill. This time we had no fear of losing her.

"Are we going home now?" Lila asked.

"Not yet," Zleta said. "First we must stop at Caleb's house."

I stared at her. "Caleb the cab driver? The one who took Dupree away and left you behind?"

"Don't worry. That was Aunt's doing, not his." She smiled. "Caleb absolutely adores me. He'll do anything I ask — especially now. He must feel very bad about abandoning me."

We turned on Benton Street and then into a narrow alley. Its walls were coated with layers of graffiti and peeling paint. Rotten vegetables, plastic bags, cans, and soda cups littered the pavement. We picked our way along, lifting our paws high, but we couldn't avoid stepping in the muck.

"I wish I'd remembered to ask Aunt for shoes," Zleta muttered.

The alley ended in a dreary courtyard lit by the moon. Rusty fire escapes zigzagged down dingy walls. Windows were either boarded up or broken. Some were even barred. Three stained plastic lawn chairs huddled by a dented metal door.

A skinny cat glared at us and vanished down a smaller alley. It might have been Nine. If it was, she'd already forgotten us.

Pigeons roosted on fire escapes and perched on windowsills, cooing to themselves. Their excrement splattered everything, even the plastic chairs. They watched us with an interest that made me uncomfortable.

Zleta knocked on the metal door. "Caleb?" she called. "It's Zleta. Are you there?"

The door opened a crack and the cab driver peered out. "Zleta," he cried. "It's really you!"

19

WE FOLLOWED ZLETA into a dark room that smelled of dirt and garbage and cigarettes, mixed in with the lovely smell of mice. The moonlight coming through one dirty window barely lit the place.

"Excuse the mess." Caleb waved his hand vaguely. Stacks of newspapers lined the walls. Books lay in piles on the floor. Dozens of black plastic bags stuffed with I couldn't imagine what filled the corners.

Zleta looked around for a place to sit, but every chair had something in it—clothing, books, shoes, and unidentifiable odds and ends.

Caleb moved the stuff from one chair and offered Zleta a seat. "If I'd known you were coming, I'd have cleaned up," Caleb said. "Maybe even baked a cake." He laughed at his own joke.

Zleta shrugged. "I've come to ask a favor, just a small one."

"I'd do anything for you, Zleta. I can't tell you how sorry I am for leaving you behind that night. You know how *she* is. I had no choice."

"It's all right, Caleb. I understand."

"I've been so worried about you. I drove all over town looking for you." He seized her hands and held them tightly. "You're as beautiful as always." When he let her go, he noticed us for the first time. "Are these her cats?"

"Yes, they're quite devoted to me."

"But it's nighttime. Shouldn't they be girls?"

Zleta sighed. "That's another story. Now I need to ask that favor."

"Even if it's the moon you want, I'll do my best to drag it down to earth for you."

Zleta laughed. "Oh, it's nothing like that, Caleb. I need a no-harm trap big enough for an animal about the size of a large cat. Also a shovel, a trowel, gardening shears, a basket, and a pair of heavy work gloves."

She paused to think. "I believe that's all. Can you get them for me?"

He looked surprised. "A trap? What on earth do you want a trap for? And the gardening stuff—what's that about?"

"Well, now, Caleb, that's really none of your business." Zleta's voice lost its honey. "Can you get it or not?"

"Sorry, didn't mean to be nosy. You just took me by surprise. Home Depot's got everything you need. Should I deliver them to Miss Dupree's new house?"

"No indeed. This is our secret, Caleb." She crossed her legs and leaned back in the chair. Her bare feet were muddy and her soles were black. "The animal I'm after lives in the woods near the ruins of the house. Can you bring the things to the old place?"

"No problem." He smiled at her. "Who's paying for it?"

"Aunt will take care of the bill. But don't give it to her right away. Wait a couple of days."

Caleb scratched his beard like he wasn't quite sure about the deal.

"What's wrong, Caleb? Aunt has always paid generously for your services."

"It's just that she hasn't paid me for mailing those boxes of clothes, and I'm running low on cash."

"Deal with it, Caleb. Open a charge account or something. You're a smart guy." She patted his cheek and smiled. "I'll expect you tomorrow at ten a.m. Enter from the back road like you did before and leave the order by the foundation."

"Will do." Caleb smoothed his hair back into his man bun. "Now that our business is settled, would you like some refreshments? I have your favorite herbal tea."

"No thanks, Caleb. I must be on my way." Zleta opened the door to let herself out. "Just a reminder. Not a word to Aunt about this. It's a surprise."

He looked at her longingly. "Will I see you tomorrow?"

"If I'm seen lurking in the ruins, I'll be questioned about the disappearance of those pesky girls. The police are desperate to find them."

"Oh, yeah, I remember them. They're still missing, right?"

"In a manner of speaking," Zleta said.

"Weird the way they just vanished. Like aliens took them or something."

"That's possible, but not probable."

Caleb didn't seem sure what Zleta meant, but he grinned anyhow, showing a mouthful of crooked teeth. "The next time I see you, I'll fix that pot of tea, along with those pretty pastries you love."

"Wonderful. You're the best friend a girl could have."

We left in a hurry, glad to be out of Caleb's house, and scurried after Zleta. She strode ahead, her hair silver in the moonlight, her black clothing indistinct in the shadows.

When we were near the ruins, Zleta said good night.

"Where are you sleeping?" I asked.

"I have no choice but to rough it, Zoey."

Lila was stunned. "You mean you're sleeping outside? You don't even have a blanket!"

"Don't worry about me. Now that I'm myself again, a night on the cold, hard ground will be uncomfortable, but nothing to fear."

Before we left, she said, "Come early tomorrow. We have much to do."

She started to walk away but turned back. "Bring me something for breakfast. Not those little packets of salmon and broth but bread and whatever else you can carry."

We watched her disappear into the dark.

"Why does she want a trap big enough for a large cat?" I asked.

"To catch us for Miss Dupree," Lila whispered in her scared kitten voice.

"No. If she wanted to do that," I said, "she'd have gone to Caleb without us, so we wouldn't suspect anything."

"Tomorrow." Nia spoke up, her voice loud in the silence. "We need to watch Zleta. We can't be sure of anything she says or does. Not for a second."

———

At ten o'clock the next morning, we sat in the ruins and watched Caleb deliver Zleta's order. Everything except the shovel and the trap fit in several Home Depot plastic bags.

We got a better look at Caleb in the sunlight. He must have been almost thirty, tall and skinny, with a sort of droopy way of standing and walking. His jeans were baggy and saggy. His faded T-shirt had a big rip on the shoulder. He wore ragged running shoes. The left one had a hole in the toe. In no way was the poor guy Zleta's type.

He hung around for a while, probably hoping Zleta would miraculously appear. After he finally gave up and drove away, Zleta stepped out of the woods and examined the trap. It looked just like the one animal control had taken away except it was new and shiny.

"Perfect." She grabbed the handle and lifted it. "Not too heavy, either."

"Why do you need a trap?" Nia asked.

"It's not for you, if that's what you're thinking." She carried it into the ruins.

Nia muttered, "If not to trap us, then who? Or what?"

Mystified, we followed Zleta. She set the trap down with a thump in what was left of the room of change and went back for the bags and the shovel.

"Help me find a level place," she said.

Lila and I paced the dirt with Zleta until we found what she wanted.

"Yes, this is perfect." The sun lit the space and cast shadows in the corners.

Next, Zleta picked up several straight sticks.

"What do you need those for?" Lila asked.

"To draw a witch's circle—something else I need hands for." She rubbed the sticks on a rough stone until they had sharp points. Then, she slowly drew a circle. Its outline was shaky and lopsided.

Zleta studied her work. "Too bad you're still a cat, Nia. You could draw a better circle than this. But no matter. Witches in the olden days must have made similar crooked ones."

She got back to work and made a pretty good copy of the large circle that had been painted on the floor of the changing room—three concentric circles with a small circle in the middle. Kind of like a geometry problem. "Not perfect but good enough."

"Last night you said the circle was just for show," I said.

"Maybe I was wrong, Maybe my spell would have worked if I'd drawn it. Maybe it would have worked if we'd had the dresses."

She looked at us. "Did the dresses burn in the fire or did you hide them away somewhere?"

"We have them," Lila said. "but we're so not giving them to you."

I was with Lila on this one. I'd read enough selkie stories to know what happens if someone steals your seal skin: you're trapped forever as a human being and can never return to the sea. Maybe the dresses were our selkie skins.

Zleta sighed loudly. "You still don't trust me! We'll need your dresses tonight."

"Fine," Nia said. "We'll bring them with us and hold on to them until Dupree comes."

"All right, all right, but please don't forget them. Tonight we must do everything right. No shortcuts."

Zleta paced around the circle. She studied the trap and the springs that controlled the door. She lifted the door, she lowered it, smiling to see it go up and down smoothly and silently. "So simple now but so impossible when I was a cat."

She frowned. "I'm forgetting something," she said. "What else do I need?"

Since Zleta hadn't told us the details of her plan, we had no idea what she'd forgotten.

A cricket chirped, and Nia pounced on it. Lila and I played Ping-Pong with a stag beetle, batting it back and forth to each other.

Zleta startled us by crying out, "That's it! Yes, of course. How could I forget? Come," she called. "I need your help."

Lila gave the beetle one last swat and watched it crawl away, dazed but still alive. I yawned, and Nia ate her cricket. It made a horrible sound.

Zleta put the garden shears and the work gloves into the basket and led us deep into the woods behind Miss Dupree's house. Even in the shade, it was hot and humid. Our fleas multiplied and bit us mercilessly.

The trees grew taller and broader here, older than the ones nearer the house. Lichen mottled their trunks and ivy clung to them, climbing up, up, and disappearing into a tangle of branches.

Crows peered down from their high perches and scolded us. *Where's the witch?* they seemed to cry. *Where's the witch?*

Zleta shook her fist at them. "Stop that racket. You don't own these woods."

The crows rose from their branches, their voices loud and harsh, and disappeared in the trees.

"A plague on them," Zleta muttered. "They wouldn't dare make a fuss if Aunt were here." She walked on, pushing brambles aside, ducking under low branches, searching for something all the while.

Brambles scratched our faces. We stepped on things that hurt our paws. I thought of the huntsman who led Snow White away from the castle to kill her. I couldn't remember what happened to her. There were dwarves, I thought, but were they good or bad?

I tugged at Zleta's skirt to get her attention. "Where are you taking us?"

"You'll see."

On we went. What choice did we have? We had no idea where we were. For all we knew, she was leading us in circles.

"Are you sure you know where you're going?" Nia asked.

"Of course." Zleta bent down to sniff a particularly nasty-smelling plant and backed away. "It's not far now."

She took a few steps one way, a few more another way, and poked at a clump of weeds. "I've found it," she cried. "Aunt's secret garden!"

To me, Miss Dupree's garden was just another patch of weeds in the deep shade of the woods. The earth was damp and smelled musty. Many of the plants grew close to the mossy ground. Their foliage was dark and smelled bad, their blossoms small and white. Others were tall and slender. I recognized foxglove from Aunt Alice's garden. Near it, I spotted delphinium and bleeding heart, also in my aunt's garden. There was even a row of lilies of the valley, one of my favorites.

Zleta frowned. "It doesn't take long for weeds to take over, does it? Aunt tended these plants every day, but she's been gone for a week. Or is it a month? I was a cat for so long, I can't remember time. Days, weeks, months, years . . . they're all jumbled."

Zleta pulled on the work gloves and walked into the garden, taking care not to brush against the plants. She examined each one as if she were shopping for vegetables in a grocery store.

When the basket was full, Zleta pointed at each plant. "Foxglove, lilies of the valley, delphinium, deadly nightshade, belladonna, bleeding heart, monkshood, and white snakeroot. Deadly poison, every one of them."

I stared at the plants in horror. "But Aunt Alice has foxglove, lilies of the valley, bleeding heart, and delphiniums in her garden. They're beautiful. How can they be poisonous?"

Zleta looked at me. "I thought you knew by now that beauty is dangerous. It can never be trusted."

"But we sing about lilies of the valley in Girl Scouts," Lila said. "You must know the song, Zoey. It starts 'White coral bells,' and something or other, and then it goes on about lilies of the valley and bells ringing . . . I can't remember exactly, but I'm sure you know the song."

"I have no idea what you're talking about, Lila. We didn't have Girl Scouts in Brooklyn. Or at least I don't think we did. Maybe though . . ." A vague image of a green vest and badges drifted into my head but disappeared before I recognized it. I shivered. Was I beginning to lose my girl memories?

Lila leaned close to sniff the lilies, but Zleta nudged her away with her foot. "Don't touch or taste anything that grows here. Some can kill you if you touch them."

"Are you going to poison someone?" Nia asked.

"Maybe, maybe not. It all depends."

"Depends on what?" I asked.

"How someone behaves." Turning her back to the poison garden, she led us through the woods to the ruins.

Still wearing the gardening gloves, Zleta crushed some of the flowers between two stones. Next she lit three dusty citronella candles, which I was sure I'd seen on my aunt's picnic table. She let them burn until the wax was soft. Blowing out the flames, she carefully pressed the crushed flowers into the wax.

"Two candles to put her to sleep," Zleta murmured, "and one to wake her up.

"Now for the last step." She selected a variety of plants and wove them into five small wreaths.

"What are they for?" Nia asked.

"You'll see." Zleta looked pleased with herself. "I've thought of everything. Our certain someone will be *my* servant tonight. I wonder how she'll like that."

She surveyed the three of us and smiled her toothy smile. "Now run along home and eat something. Take a nap if you like, but come back this afternoon."

20

AUNT ALICE WAS SITTING on the back steps, doing a crossword puzzle. She looked like she'd been crying. Nia and Lila went inside, but I leapt into her lap. While she stroked me, she found bits and pieces of the woods. A twig here, a leaf there, and dozens of those little green, sticky things called beggar's lice.

"If I had a cat cam," she said, "I'd hang it around your neck and see what you do in the woods. I imagine you hunt for mice and shrews and voles, but I hope you don't eat them."

Aunt Alice parted the fur on the nape of my neck and examined my skin. "Yep, you have fleas, Miss Jenny. If you're eating mice, you probably have worms as well."

"I don't eat mice," I meowed. "I'm not a cat! And my name isn't Jenny!"

She caressed me gently. "Oh, Jenny, I don't know what to do. The police came again today to tell us they have no leads. They don't know who took Zoey and Lila or where they are. My sister and I are devastated. I'm tired and scared, and so is she."

A tear splashed down on my head. I stood on my hind legs

and licked her face. If only I could tell her I'd be myself tonight. In just a few hours, she and Mom were going to be so happy. I tingled all over just thinking about it.

———

Later in the afternoon, we went back to the ruins to see what Zleta was up to. We found her bent over the shovel, digging a hole. Her T-shirt was soaked through with sweat, and her feet and legs were caked with mud. Her hair was a frizzy mess. For the first time, she actually looked like a real person.

She must have heard us sneaking up on her because she whirled around and glared at us. Her face was as dirty as the rest of her. "Don't you ever spy on me again!"

Lila and I stayed where we were, but Nia sauntered over and peered into the hole. "Who are you planning to bury?"

"I'm not burying anyone. I'm digging something up." She wiped her forehead with the back of her hand and smeared more mud across her face. "The ground's solid clay, heavy as lead, and full of roots. It's taking forever."

"What are you digging for?" Nia asked.

"I buried something here, and now I need it."

"What is it? Why do you need it?"

"Surely you know curiosity kills cats."

"And surely you know cats have nine lives."

For a moment, I expected Zleta to lash her tail and hiss, but no, she was human now and had other ways to express herself.

"You aren't as clever as you think, Nia." With that, she turned her back and kept on digging. The shovel clunked against something. She dropped to her knees and peered into the hole. "That's it, I see it!"

She began digging with her bare hands, as if she'd forgotten she was human. Lila and I helped her. Between her fingers and our claws, we freed a corner of a box that Zleta struggled to pull out of the ground.

I expected to see a treasure chest, but the box was metal, totally ordinary, and very rusty, its sides caked with mud.

Zleta pried it open. Lila moved closer to me. We held our breath. What was inside? Was it dangerous?

But all we saw was a carefully folded black shawl.

She touched the shawl and smiled. "In this box are the things I need to survive without Aunt."

She laid the shawl carefully aside. Leaning over the box, she pointed to the things inside. "A very expensive Dupree dress made of pure silk," she said, "a pair of her finest shoes, a purse made of ostrich skin, very chic, very costly."

She smiled as she showed us what was in the purse. "My passport, my birth certificate, my diploma from a good college, my driver's license, and my social security card. Oh, yes, Aunt helped me acquire what I needed to travel with her. All fake, of course, but done so well no one has ever questioned any of them. Caleb isn't just a cab driver, you know. He's also a highly skilled forger.

"But this, *this* is real." Zleta showed us what filled the bottom of the purse—dozens of rolls of hundred-dollar bills. "You're looking at fifty thousand dollars."

None of us had ever seen that much money. Lila and I touched it with our paws. We even sniffed it. Fifty thousand dollars.

"What did you do?" Nia asked. "Rob a bank?"

"No, nothing like that. Aunt put me in charge of her finances. She loved being rich but managing money bored her, so she left it all to me." Zleta looked proud of herself. "I took a little here and a little there. She never noticed."

She stood up, the box clasped close to her filthy T-shirt. "Now," she said. "I need a bath and a shampoo. If you'll bring me a bar of soap, I'll use the outside shower behind your garage. How considerate of your aunt to provide it."

Zleta ran across the lawn so fast we saw nothing but a blur.

"What a cool way not to be seen," Lila said. "It's almost like being invisible."

Nia twitched her tail. "That's what I mean. We have to keep an eye on her all the time."

Aunt Alice and Mom were on the front porch talking to Lila's mother, so it was easy to snitch a bar of soap from the kitchen sink. I carried it in my mouth. It tasted so nasty I almost threw up. Nia and Lila yanked a towel from the clothesline in the back-yard. Nia took one corner in her teeth and Lila another. Together they dragged the towel to the outdoor shower hidden behind a trellis covered with trumpet vines.

Aunt Alice used the shower to clean up after a day of hard work in the garden. She claimed cold water was better for you on a hot day. I refused to use it, but Zleta didn't seem to mind the water's temperature. She hummed a strange tune and took her time.

When she finally came out of the shower, she wore the black silk dress and red sandals. The purse dangled from her shoulder. Her dress rustled and her hair shone in the sunlight.

She was as glamorous as ever — and maybe even more dangerous.

"I am beautiful again." Zleta smiled as if she expected us to be happy to see her old self — the lying, two-faced Zleta, Miss Dupree's partner in witchcraft.

"Keep your eye on her. She's as treacherous as a snake," Nia whispered to me.

Still smiling, Zleta told us to meet her in the ruins after dark. "We have things to do before Aunt arrives."

The next thing we knew, she was waving to us from the woods on the other side of the yard.

Lila watched Zleta merge with the shadows. "I wish I knew how to do that."

"Me too," I said.

When we came home, Aunt Alice put down three bowls of food. Still holding a fourth bowl, she looked at us. "Where is Queenie?"

Even if we'd told her in plain English, she wouldn't have believed us, so we kept our heads down and ate our food as if we were ordinary cats.

Aunt Alice set Zleta's bowl on the counter and went to the kitchen door. "Queenie, kitty, kitty, kitty."

She called several times. Mom came downstairs and joined her. "Is that cat gone already?"

"I hope not. Such a beautiful girl, so sweet. I never knew how much comfort cats can be."

"I won't miss her," Mom said. "She struck me as sly and sneaky, much more devious than most cats. But then I'm not fond of Persians. Too much fur and not enough nose. They always look smug, like they know something I don't know."

Mom was right about that—Zleta knew things Mom couldn't imagine. I rubbed against her, but as usual she ignored me.

Aunt Alice picked me up and cuddled me. "You and Missy and Nia will stay with us, won't you?"

I purred as loudly as I could. "Yes," I said, "yes, we'll stay with you—as girls or cats, we'll be here." *Please let it be girls,* I thought, *please, please, please* . . .

Mom watched her sister fussing over me. "I don't like black cats, either," she said. "In fact, the only cat I've ever tolerated is Suki. She's a Siamese and highly intelligent."

Suki—there was that name again. A cat, a Siamese, highly intelligent. Why didn't I remember her?

After dinner, Mom went to her room to read and Alice sat on the porch to watch the sun set. I sat beside her trying to remember the name of my favorite movie. It was about a girl lost in a strange world, and she wanted to go home. How did it end? Did she ever see her mom and dad?

Aunt Alice stroked my head in a very soothing way. I purred and purred. My mind slipped away from Suki and the movie. I let them go. I let Brooklyn go. I let our apartment and pizza and ice cream go. Those things belonged in someone else's story.

"Look, Jenny." Aunt Alice nudged me awake. "It's the evening star. Zoey always made a wish on it, but she'd never tell me what it was. Wishes are like secrets—if you talk about them, they never come true."

Wishes. Yes, I remembered wishes. There was a poem you were supposed to say, something about a first star, but of course I'd forgotten how it went. I didn't know which was the right star, so I looked at the whole sky and made my wish.

When Lila, Nia, and I left the house that night, the wind was high in the treetops. The moon slipped in and out of clouds as it followed us through the woods. We ran with each other, flowing like shadows through the trees, excited by the sounds and smells.

Lila bounced ahead, batting at lightning bugs. Circling back to me, she said, "Soon we'll be girls, maybe in just a few hours. What's the first thing you want to do?"

"Talk! I want to talk! I want to hug Mom, hug Aunt Alice, and tell them how much I love them. I want to see my mother smile. I want to hear her laugh."

Lila gave me a cat high-five. "Yes! Talk, hug Mom and Dad. Sleep in my own bed. Just be me again!"

The two of us babbled on and on about bicycles and books and hamburgers, cat-laughing so hard we could hardly talk.

After I'd run out of things to talk about, I noticed Nia hadn't said a word. "How about you?" I asked. "What do you want to do when —"

She interrupted me. "I'm not making any plans until I really am a girl."

"What do you mean?" I looked at her, suddenly fearful.

Nia stared into the darkness. "So many things can go wrong. What if Dupree is stronger than Zleta thinks? What if Zleta changes sides? What if we end up in Dupree's power again?"

Lila edged away from Nia. "Why do you always ruin things? Can't we be happy without you getting all gloomy?"

Although I was definitely on Lila's side this time, the dark part of me whispered, *Nia could be right. Don't hope for anything until it happens.*

Her head down, Nia walked toward the ruins. We followed her slowly, our heads down like hers, our tails drooping, our happy mood gone.

Zleta was waiting in the shadows. The moon lit her hair and her face. The rest of her was hidden in darkness.

"You look frightened," Zleta said. "And worried. Share a drink with me. Milk and honey and a little mint. It will give you courage."

I didn't know where she'd gotten them, but she set three bowls on the ground. A delicious aroma rose from the creamy liquid. For herself, Zleta had a glass full of the same drink.

Nia turned up her nose. "Milk gives me a bellyache. It's not good for cats." She looked at us. "You shouldn't drink it either."

Lila stuck her nose in the bowl and sniffed. "It smells yummy. It won't hurt us."

I sniffed too and took a sip. "Nia, it's delicious. Try it!"

"I don't want it. I'm not thirsty. I'm not hungry. And I hate milk."

"You're just being a gloomy old grouch as usual, trying to spoil everything."

Zleta raised her glass. "Drink it or leave it. It makes no difference to me." She finished hers in a few swallows and smiled at us.

Lila and I polished ours off. It was sweet and creamy and tasted better than anything else I'd drunk as a cat. In fact, it tasted so good, we shared Nia's bowl. I was pretty sure I felt brave enough now to face Miss Dupree.

"Aunt will be here soon," Zleta said. "We must prepare for her. Hide behind the trap and mew pitifully. Aunt has to think you're actually in the trap. Beg me to let you out. Beg me to forgive you."

"I don't beg," Nia said.

"I'll beg," Lila said. "I'll beg enough for all of us."

"Me too. I'll beg," I said.

Zleta frowned at Nia. "Perhaps you'll meow?"

"Perhaps," Nia said.

"All right then." Zleta took a deep breath. "Stay out of sight and do what I say. Do you understand?"

Lila and I said we understood. Nia lashed her tail.

"Where are your dresses?"

In our excitement, we'd forgotten all about them.

"Quick," Zleta said. "We don't have much time. Show me where they are!"

With her close behind, we ran to Aunt Alice's yard and dove under the forsythia bush. The dresses were where we'd left them, a little damp, a little dirty and wrinkled, but safe.

With Zleta carrying our dresses, we hurried back to the ruins. After she'd hidden the dresses behind the trap, she told us to stay with them. "Remember what I told you: cry and beg me to free you. Make it sound like you're in the trap."

We watched Zleta pace back and forth. She seemed worried. Maybe she thought Miss Dupree wouldn't come. Maybe her plan wouldn't fool the witch. Maybe Miss Dupree had more power than Zleta thought.

We were worried too. Also scared. If Zleta failed, what would Miss Dupree do to us?

"She should have another glass of milk," Lila whispered.

"We should too." That made us both laugh so much Zleta gave us each a slap on the head. "Be quiet," she said. "She'll come soon. Go and hide behind the trap."

We stopped laughing. "She didn't have to slap us," Lila muttered.

Nia sat a few feet away from us, her back turned, twitching her tail. *She must be mad at us*, I thought, *for drinking the milk*. Sometimes Lila was right about Nia being bossy.

21

SUDDENLY ZLETA RAISED A FINGER as if she were testing the wind. "I smell her. Not a sound from you, not a movement."

My bravery popped like a bubble, and Lila and I huddled together and shook with fear. Nia crouched beside us and growled softly.

"Dear, sweet Aunt," Zleta cried. "Thank you for coming."

I peeked around the trap and saw the ugly, long-legged black cat I'd last seen getting into Caleb's taxi. Even as a cat, Miss Dupree looked bad. Her fur was dingy and dull and stood up along her spine. She was the very image of a Halloween cat, the sort people dreaded to see crossing the road ahead of them.

Lila's teeth chattered. Nia continued to growl. I drew back and closed my eyes. I didn't want to see Miss Dupree or hear her voice.

Lila nudged me. It was time to play our parts. "Let us out, Zleta," we begged. "Don't let Miss Dupree take us. Please, please."

Nia didn't beg but meowed like a scared cat.

"We trusted you, Zleta," I cried. "How could you do this to us?"

"Where are they?" Miss Dupree asked. "I hear them but I don't see them."

"Come, I'll show you." Zleta led her to the trap.

Still in her cat body, Miss Dupree crouched and squinted into the shadows. "I smell them, but I still don't see them."

Behind the witch's back, Zleta reached into her pocket, pulled out a live mouse, and tossed it into the trap.

Miss Dupree pounced on the mouse and the door slammed shut behind her. She threw herself at the door. It shuddered under her weight but did not open.

"You traitor!" Miss Dupree screamed at Zleta. "Let me out immediately! I command you!"

Zleta smiled the sort of smile only your worst enemy gives you. "Now it's *you* who must obey *me!*" she cried. Turning to us, she said, "Show yourselves to your old friend."

Still frightened of Miss Dupree, we crept to Zleta's side and stared at the raging cat in the trap. She hurled herself at the door over and over again, but the trap had been made to catch big strong animals. No way was she getting out.

When she saw us, Miss Dupree lashed her tail. She bared her teeth and slashed the air with her claws.

"You're going to be sorry for this, Zleta! When I get out — and I *will* get out — I'll turn you and your new friends into slugs and eat you for dinner."

"Why doesn't she magic herself out of the trap?" Lila asked Zleta.

"She needs to be human to do that. Unfortunately, poor dear

Aunt doesn't have what she needs to change. No candle, no circle." Zleta laughed.

Turning her back on the furious cat, Zleta lit two of the three candles and placed one on each side of the trap.

"Come away," she told us. "Or the scent will put you to sleep."

Already drowsy, we followed her out of the ruins to where the air was fresh.

Lila sniffed and yawned. "Those candles smell like the perfume you used to wear."

Zleta smiled. "Yes, I suppose they do."

In the trap, Miss Dupree twisted and writhed as if she meant to turn herself inside out.

Zleta laughed again. "Oh, it does my wicked heart good to see her suffer."

Nia turned her large cat eyes to Zleta. "For maybe the first time ever, I agree with you."

"You don't feel even a tiny bit sorry for her?" Lila asked.

"After all that witch has done? No, I don't feel the tiniest bit of pity," Nia said. "And you shouldn't, either."

Lila looked at me. She'd put her paws over her ears to block Miss Dupree's cries. "What about you, Zoey?"

"I just wish she'd shut up before Aunt Alice hears her and thinks Queenie's in trouble. What would she do if she saw what we're doing?"

Lila looked like she couldn't imagine what my aunt might do. I wasn't sure, either, but I had a feeling she'd put a stop to it.

"Don't worry," Zleta said. "The candles are working. She'll be asleep soon."

Sure enough, the shrieks of anger slowly faded, and the woods were quiet. So quiet, I heard Mom and Aunt Alice talking on the back porch.

"It's stopped," Aunt Alice said. "I hope it wasn't Queenie."

"Maybe it was a fisher cat," Mom said. "They screech like that."

The back door closed and the light in the kitchen went out. A few minutes later the light upstairs also went out. I pictured Mom getting into bed. I ached to be there with her, not as a cat, but as myself.

Zleta beckoned to us. "It's time for the part you've been waiting for."

Putting on the work gloves, she opened the trap's door, pulled out the unconscious cat, and laid her in the inner circle. Next she twisted the wreaths of flowers around the cat's four legs and pulled another over her head. Last of all, she sprinkled some sort of evil-smelling powder around the circle's edge.

Stepping back, she smiled down at the cat. "There. You have no power except what I give you."

Turning to us, she said, "Take your places in the circle, Nia in space thirteen, Zoey in fourteen, and Lila in fifteen."

She laid our folded dresses in front of us and placed the third citronella candle beside Miss Dupree. "This one will wake her up."

A few moments after Zleta lit the candle, Miss Dupree began to stir and stretch. At first, she looked about, merely puzzled about where she was and how she'd gotten there.

She made an effort to stand up. On four wobbly paws, she examined the wreaths.

Then she understood. She tried to bite them off, but the poison burned her lips and she spat. She ran to the edge of the circle and fell backward. "You!" she screamed at Zleta. "Traitor! Release me!"

"I don't think so," Zleta said. "Our roles have reversed in my favor. I like that."

In her strange language, Miss Dupree hurled what were most likely curses at Zleta. They had no effect, perhaps because of the small corsage of plants Zleta had pinned to her dress.

Miss Dupree wound down with a series of hisses. "What do you want from me?"

"First, these two girls," Zleta said. "After you betrayed me, Fourteen and Fifteen were very helpful to me. You must end their suffering by changing them to the girls they were before you got hold of them. They must be allowed to live their lives as humans without fearing you."

"And what of Thirteen?"

"Thirteen is a problem I haven't solved. She's been rude, distrustful, disobedient, dishonest—vexatious beyond all patience. She has two choices: apologize and become a girl like the other two, or remain a cat forever."

Lila cried out in fright, "Nia, please apologize!"

I stared at Lila. "Of course she'll apologize. She's too smart not to."

But Nia lashed her tail and said, "I don't apologize to people who wrong me."

Zleta frowned. "Be careful. If you refuse to apologize, you will remain a cat for the rest of your natural life."

"I've been thinking," Nia said. "I'll never find my way home. I don't even know where I used to live. I don't remember my parents' names. I don't remember my name. I feel more like a cat than a person. Why not stay as I am?"

Lila moved toward Nia. "You can't mean that!"

"Please, Nia," I begged. "Don't stay a cat. Apologize to her. You can come back to New York with Mom and me or stay here with Lila or Aunt Alice. You'll have a home, I promise!"

"You can be an artist," Lila cried. "You can design your own fashions or paint whatever you want you to!"

Nia shook her head.

"Enough chatter," Zleta said. "Go back to your places. You heard Thirteen. She might regret her choice later, but no apology, no change. She stays a cat. Simple as that."

While we'd talked, the ugly black cat had listened, turning her head like someone at a tennis match watching the ball fly back and forth across the net. Every now and then, she muttered to herself.

Zleta looked at the witch. "Are you ready to change Lila and Zoey, Aunt?"

"As a cat?" She lashed her tail, the only part of her not bound with wreaths. "I need to be myself to do magic. Change me, and I'll change Fourteen and Fifteen. Thirteen can stay as she is. I'll put her in the trap and take her with me when we're done here."

"No!" I cried. "Apologize, Nia, please. Don't let Miss Dupree take you away with her!"

Nia licked her paw and washed her face. "Don't worry. I'll get away from her again."

"You want me to change you to your evil, ugly self?" Zleta looked at Miss Dupree and laughed. "Oh, Aunt, do you take me for a fool? Change the girls as you are now. You have the circle, the candles, and the words to say. I know you can do it." She smiled the terrible smile again. "Afterward, we'll discuss the terms for your release."

"If I change those horrid girls, what's to stop them from telling their parents who took them and where they've been?"

"I've already thought of that, Aunt. Once they become girls, they won't remember what happened to them or where they've been. All it takes is a spell for forgetfulness. People will think they have amnesia brought on by post-traumatic stress disorder. Perhaps you've heard of it?"

A spell? When did that happen? Was it something we smelled, something she said? Then I remembered the drink Zleta gave us. I glanced at Nia. She'd warned us, but we hadn't listened to her. We hadn't been careful.

Miss Dupree's tail lashed savagely. "I must say you've been an excellent pupil, Zleta. If I'd known how clever you are, I'd have kept my magic to myself."

"Flattery will get you nowhere, as someone famous must once have said." Zleta stood straighter and brushed her hair out of her face. "Now," she told Miss Dupree. "Get busy."

"You will free me to change myself afterward?" Miss Dupree's voice quavered.

Her power seemed to be draining away before our eyes. Maybe it had something to do with the wreaths. Or maybe Zleta was transferring Miss Dupree's power to herself, for surely she was taller, stronger, and lots more confident.

"Of course, dearest Aunt, of course. We will be a team again, you and I—I promise you."

Miss Dupree rose unsteadily to her hind legs and began the changing chant. I didn't dare look at the witch or at anyone else. Closing my eyes tightly, I whispered, "Please let it work, please make Lila and me girls again."

I'd been a cat longer than the last time I changed, so I guessed that was why it hurt so much more than I remembered. Pain shot through my body. My bones seemed to catch fire, my muscles melted. In agony, I felt my shape shift, change, grow taller. Just as I thought I couldn't stand another second of it, the pain stopped. I opened my eyes slowly, fearful of what I'd see.

And there I was—arms, hands, legs, all of me, furless, clawless, tailless.

Next to me was Lila, no longer a cat but the girl I'd known before we ended up in Miss Dupree's house.

22

CRYING TEARS OF RELIEF, we fumbled for our dresses, struggled to put them on, tried to stand up, but sat back down, too weak to balance our weight on two legs.

Nearby, a small black cat watched us stagger to our feet again. This time we didn't fall but stood shakily.

That was when the strangeness started. Lila and I were in the ruins of a burned house, surrounded by trees. It was night. Dark. The moon drifted in and out of clouds. Deep in the woods, an owl called. I had no idea where we were or how we'd gotten there. Lila reached for my hand and held it tightly.

We weren't alone. A beautiful woman with blond hair stood in the middle of a badly drawn, lopsided circle. She wore a fashionable black dress and red high heels. A black bag with a long strap hung from her shoulder, and in one hand, she held an animal trap. Inside was a yowling black cat.

The woman looked completely out of place. What was she doing in the woods dressed like that? What were we doing here? Was this an especially realistic dream or what?

"Who are you?" Lila whispered to the woman. "Where are we?"

The mysterious woman smiled. "What are you waiting for? Don't you want to go home?"

Yes, of course, that was exactly what Lila and I wanted to do. But where was home? Which way?

And then I remembered: Lila and I were in Miss Dupree's woods. We'd been at my aunt's house watching *Bewitched,* our favorite TV show, when we'd heard a cat yowling in the dark. We'd gone outside to find it, but after five, maybe ten minutes, we'd given up the search. The night was chilly and our feet were cold, so we'd started walking back home. But we'd seen something strange.

I turned to Lila. "Who was that woman with the animal cage?"

"What woman?"

"There was only one, Lila. She was beautiful — blond hair, black dress, red shoes. You didn't see her?"

She shook her head. "Is this a joke or what?"

"Are you gaslighting me?"

"Of course not. You must have imagined it, Zoey."

"No. I saw her, I swear it."

"Very weird, very strange." Lila grabbed my arm. "Come on, let's go home. I'm cold."

We ran out of the woods just as an old black taxi sped past us. A passenger waved to us from the back seat, but all I saw was a cloud of silvery-blond hair.

"Who was that?" Lila asked.

"It was her, the woman I saw, in the back seat of that cab."

"This is crazy," Lila said. "I'll see you tomorrow. Maybe we can talk your aunt into going to the swimming pool!"

Still puzzled, I watched Lila run across the street to her house. How could she not have seen the mysterious woman? We'd been together the whole time. If I'd seen her, Lila should have seen her too. Unless—scary thought—I was hallucinating or something.

A small black cat meowed and nudged my legs. I bent down to pet her. "Well, where did you come from?"

She followed me to my aunt's house and watched me turn the doorknob. To my surprise, it was locked. Had Aunt Alice forgotten I'd gone outside to find that cat in the woods?

I rang the bell. Still no one came. I rang it again and again. Where was my aunt? Why was it taking her so long to come to the door?

Finally the porch light flashed on, and a voice called, "Who's there?"

It sounded like Mom, but how could that be? She was in Brooklyn.

"Open the door. It's me, Zoey."

The door flew open and my mother stared at me in astonishment. "Zoey," she cried. "Zoey, oh my lord, is it really you?"

She grabbed me and hugged me and started to cry. Aunt Alice ran out and joined in the hugging. They carried on as if I'd been gone for days, weeks, years. It was totally insane. And actually pretty scary.

I tried to pull away, but they held me even more tightly. What was wrong with them? Had they lost their minds? Something had shifted and nothing seemed quite right.

At last, they dragged me into the house and started asking questions: "Where have you been? Are you all right? Has anyone hurt you?"

"Lila and I went outside to find the cat, the one yowling its head off. We were worried it was hurt or trapped or something. Don't you remember?"

"Zoey." Mom held my shoulders and stared into my eyes. "You and Lila have been missing for days. The police searched everywhere but couldn't find a trace of you. It was like you disappeared into a black hole."

She shuddered and gasped and tried to stop crying, but even though she blew her nose and wiped her eyes, the tears didn't stop. "It's been horrible," she cried. "I thought I'd never see you again!"

"I don't know what you're talking about, Mom." I stared at her, more confused than ever. "And how come you're here? You were in Brooklyn when Lila and I left the house to look for the cat. It's like everything's gone upside down and inside out in ten minutes." I turned to Aunt Alice. "If you were worried, why didn't you just call us to come home?"

Aunt Alice held my hand gently. "You really don't remember, do you, Zoey?"

"I remember everything. Lila and I went into the woods to find the cat. We weren't missing. I'm home now and so is she. What's the big deal? And how did Mom get here?"

Mom looked at me closely. "Where did you get that dress? You've never owned anything like that. And your shoes—where are they?"

I looked down at my muddy feet and the shapeless black dress. Mom was right: I'd never owned anything like it. Where had it come from? What had happened to my shorts and T-shirt? And my shoes—I loved those sneakers. Where had they gone?

Now that everybody had stopped crying, I realized I was scared. Something bad must have happened to Lila and me. Why couldn't I remember?

"I don't know why I'm wearing this dress," I whispered.

Mom stared at Aunt Alice. "Isn't there a commune in the mountains where girls wear black dresses and go barefoot? Maybe they kidnapped Zoey and Lila. And brainwashed them. Isn't that what cults do?"

"Not possible, Ellen. They're lovely people dedicated to peace and nature. The only time they come to town is to sell or barter things—homemade soap, beeswax candles, herbs, wooden toys."

Mom frowned. "I just thought—"

Aunt Alice interrupted Mom. "Don't get upset, but I think we should ask Zoey about Miss Dupree."

"Oh, for goodness' sake, Alice, no. Not that again."

Aunt Alice ignored Mom and asked, "Zoey, do you remember Miss Dupree?"

"That weird old lady next door?" I asked. "I never saw her, but I remember you talking about her. She has a lot of scuzzy black cats. And she stays in her house and never goes anywhere or talks to anybody and she has No Trespassing signs everywhere."

"Do you recall rescuing one of her cats? You named her Nia. Miss Dupree tried to get her back and scared you half to death."

I looked at the small black cat sitting at my feet. She must have followed me inside, but I was sure I'd never seen her before.

"Yes," Aunt Alice said. "That's the cat I mean. Nia."

"She's beautiful," I said, "but why would I steal her? I have a cat back home in Brooklyn. Suki."

Nia meowed and looked at me. I squatted beside her and stroked her. "Nia's a really good name for you, just the one I'd pick for a pretty cat like you."

Aunt Alice had more to say about Miss Dupree. "Are you sure she didn't take you and Lila somewhere? You thought she was a witch. She screamed at you in the street. She tried over and over to get Nia back. You were terrified of that woman and her cats. How could you forget all about it?"

Something was really wrong. Mom had folded her arms across her chest. She seemed to be very angry with Aunt Alice.

Aunt Alice herself was all intense and anxious, demanding answers I couldn't give. I'd never seen her act like this. She was always calm. Never a nervous wreck.

Close to tears, I said, "I don't know what you're talking about! I never said Miss Dupree was a witch. I never even met her. There's no such thing as witches anyway." I was tired and hungry and about to cry.

Mom glared at Aunt Alice. "Stop it! You're upsetting Zoey. I told you Miss Dupree had nothing to do with her disappearance."

Now I was angry at Aunt Alice. "If you don't believe me," I said, "why don't we go next door and ask Miss Dupree?"

Aunt Alice and Mom looked at me as if I'd said something too strange for words.

In a very calm voice, Aunt Alice said, "Miss Dupree's house burned down, Zoey. No one's seen her since."

"A fire? I don't remember a fire!" I began crying then. "Please, can't I just go to bed? I'm so tired my head hurts."

Mom put her arm around me. "Oh, my darling Zoey, you must be exhausted. Lord knows what you've been through."

Alice joined the hug. "What were we thinking, asking you all those questions? I'm so sorry. We should all go to bed and get some sleep. Maybe everything will be clear in the morning."

Mom and Aunt Alice took me to my room and tucked me into bed as if I were five years old. There was a lot more hugging and kissing, and Mom cried again.

Finally, Aunt Alice took Mom's arm and drew her away. "Let her get some sleep now. You and I could use a few hours ourselves."

Nia had followed us to my room. She curled up beside me and purred. I stroked her gently. Somehow the sound of her purr and the contours of her body felt familiar. Comforting. As if I'd spent many nights sleeping beside her.

Despite the cat's warmth, it was hard to sleep. If I didn't remember anything Aunt Alice asked me about, what memories did I have? I recalled seeing Miss Dupree's cats. The day after I arrived, I'd looked out of my bedroom window and there they were in Miss Dupree's woods. Then there was the library and meeting Lila. Something had happened between Lila and the cats, something scary, but I couldn't remember what it was. After that, it was like trying to read a message written in invisible ink on a blank page. If I couldn't see the words, how was I ever to know what had happened to Lila and me?

I struggled to make sense of it all. Things flickered through my head like fragments of dreams that never connect—the woods, the cats, Lila, Miss Dupree. Why couldn't I sort it out?

Finally I gave up on sleeping and went down the hall to crawl into bed with Mom.

"My sweet girl," she whispered. "You'll never know how I've longed for you to come back, and now here you are, walking in the door as if you'd been gone only a few minutes. Where can you have been?"

Half-asleep, I mumbled, "In the woods with the cats."

Mom hugged me. "It doesn't matter if you never remember. You're here, that's what's important."

After Mom had fallen asleep, Nia jumped on the bed beside me. I stroked her gently. "Such a soft, lovely black cat you are. I feel so close to you. It's like somehow, some way, you were with

Lila and me while we were gone." I yawned. "But how could that be?"

·   Nia purred loudly and rubbed her face against my cheek. Her eyes peered into mine. Held by her stare, I asked, "What do you see when you look at me like that?"

I almost expected her to answer, but of course she didn't. Whoever heard of a talking cat?

23

WHEN I FINALLY FELL ASLEEP, I dreamed Lila and I were cats playing in the moonlight. We chased each other, hiding and pouncing, rolling in the grass, hunting beetles and mice. It was great to feel so free in my body, so loose and stretchy, never worrying that I was clumsy or awkward, the way I felt in my human body. As a cat, I jumped high and came down lightly. I ran effortlessly, barely feeling my feet touch the ground.

In my dream, Nia joined the game. It felt so right to be together, three black cats in the moonlight.

Suddenly a big, skinny black cat joined us. Her back was humped like a Halloween cat. Her teeth were sharp, and she had a wicked look.

Lila, Nia, and I ran from her, and the Halloween cat chased us straight toward Miss Dupree's house. Faster we went, faster and faster. Behind us the Halloween cat screamed, "Now you know who I am and what I can do!" Her claws raked my back, and I woke up screaming. It was still night and my scream hung in the air for a moment, frightening Nia.

Mom held me tightly. "It's all right, Zoey. It was a dream, just a dream. I'll keep you safe. Nothing can hurt you."

I clung to her and sobbed like a child. "Oh, Mom, it was so real. The cat, the horrible cat, she . . ."

Mom stroked my hair and rocked me gently. Slowly, I stopped shaking. My heart slowed down. I breathed normally.

"There," Mom whispered, "there, there, my dear darling Zoey. Sleep now. No more bad dreams."

Her voice comforted me. Nia cuddled beside me and purred. The dream faded, and I fell asleep.

In the morning, Lila rang the doorbell before I was out of bed. I pulled on my clothes and ran downstairs to meet her.

Mom and Aunt Alice wanted to talk to us, but we escaped to the porch. Nia followed and perched on the porch railing near me. Lila and I had important things of our own to talk about.

Aunt Alice stuck her head out the door. "Hey, you two," she called. "Don't go anywhere. I called the police and they want to interview you. They should be here soon."

Lila sat close to me on the swing. "What will we tell them? We don't know anything."

"I hope they don't get mad and grill us like they do in police shows. You know, the good-cop-bad-cop routine."

"Don't worry. We're minors. Our parents will be with us."

For a while, we swung back and forth in the swing without talking. It was one of those nice summer days, warm, not hot. A breeze blew through the garden, bringing a nice smell with it. I watched the foxgloves and the delphinium sway.

"Did you know that some of the most beautiful flowers are poisonous?" I asked Zoey.

"I think I heard that somewhere. Some can kill you if you touch them."

"I had the weirdest dream last night."

"So did I," Lila said. "You tell me yours and I'll tell you mine."

"Well, you and I were cats and we were having so much fun playing together. Nia was there too." I stroked Nia, who had moved to my lap. "But all of a sudden, another cat was there, the biggest, ugliest black cat you ever saw. She chased us into the woods, straight toward Miss Dupree's house, and she was so close I heard her snapping her teeth."

When I stopped to take a breath, Lila interrupted. "And the mean ugly cat said, 'Now you know who I am and what I can do!'"

I stared at her, amazed. "Yes, that's exactly what she said. How did you know?"

"I had the exact same dream!"

I almost fell out of the swing. "Why did we dream the same dream? It must mean something."

Lila gave the swing a little push with her toe. "The really big question is: Why don't we remember being missing? We had to be somewhere. But where?"

"My brain gets all muzzy when I think about it."

"Same here."

I gave the swing a bigger push. "What's the last thing you remember?"

"Meeting you at the library and walking home through the park." She thought a moment. "Something happened in the park. Do you remember what?"

"All I remember for sure is my first day at Aunt Alice's house and seeing the cats in Miss Dupree's yard the next day. Then the library and you. There was something scary in between seeing the cats and meeting you, but I don't remember what."

I rocked the swing. "After that, everything's a big blank. We were together, you and me, I'm sure of that, but I don't remember where we were or what we did. It's like the missing days are all broken into pieces that don't fit together."

Lila pressed her fingers against her forehead. "Everything's a muddle. Nothing makes sense. What were we scared of? Who were we afraid of?"

"What if we really were kidnapped?" I asked. "And someone hypnotized us so we couldn't remember what actually happened?"

"I've seen that plot in a lot of movies," Lila said. "Books too."

I sighed. "Yeah, that's true. I doubt it ever happens in real life, but still—why can't we remember?"

The phone rang then, and Aunt Alice answered. From the porch, we heard her talking to the police. After she hung up, she called us inside. A detective was coming in half an hour to talk to us.

After the police, reporters and TV news people interviewed us. Psychiatrists and doctors examined us. They pretty much agreed we had post-traumatic stress disorder. When something bad happens to you, you want to forget it, so you get amnesia.

Facebook and Twitter went wild. Meme after meme about us popped up—alien abduction was the most popular. People on talk radio claimed we'd run away and pretended to have amnesia to keep from being punished. Someone actually spray-painted "Fake News" on Aunt Alice's sidewalk.

For a couple of weeks, reporters lurked everywhere, hoping to take our picture or interview us. Lila and I stayed home and texted each other. It was a nightmare.

Sometime in August, Mom decided we needed to go back to Brooklyn and return to a normal life.

The worst part of going home was leaving Lila. What happened to us, whatever it was, had made us best friends forever. Sisters, almost.

We had a plan, though. Since we both loved manga as well as anime, we'd write a book about two girls who turn into cats and have so much fun that they almost forget they used to be girls. We weren't sure how it would end—the girls might stay cats; they might change back to girls; they might halfway change, into girls with tails and whiskers. Since I was better at writing than drawing, I'd be the author, and Lila, who was better at drawing, would be the illustrator.

We'd video chat every Sunday to talk about the story and the pictures. We'd probably text and email too. And of course I'd be back in Bexhill next summer. So it wasn't like we'd never see each other again.

Then there was Nia. At first I begged Mom to let me take her to Brooklyn with us, but she talked me out of it. Nia was an outdoor cat. How could she be happy in the city? She'd be better off in Bexhill with Aunt Alice. Besides, I had a cat. Suppose Suki didn't like Nia?

The day I was packing to leave, Nia jumped into my suitcase. I lifted her out, and she jumped back in and curled up as if she meant to stay there.

"You wouldn't like Brooklyn," I told her. "It has lots of traffic and loud noises and people rushing along. We only have a little garden in the back and a balcony. And I have a cat at home. Suki might be jealous of you. She might hiss at you and want to fight."

Nia cocked her ears and stared at me as if she understood what I'd told her.

"You really want to go to Brooklyn?" I asked her.

She stepped gracefully out of my suitcase, purred, and rubbed her face against my face. Then she jumped back in the suitcase and continued to stare at me, as if to say, *I'm going to Brooklyn with you.*

"I wish you could come, Nia, I really do, but in Brooklyn, you'll be trapped in the apartment all day and all night. You'll never go outside again. You know you'd hate that."

Nia stared at me with her big eyes, ears perked to hear every word. Slowly she stood up, stretched, yawned, and left the suitcase. After rubbing her face against mine once more, she ran downstairs. From the window, I watched her bound across the yard and pounce on something in the flower garden.

It was just as if she'd told me I was right — she'd be happier here.

———

I don't think I'll ever remember where Lila and I were or what we did during the missing days. Maybe someday I'll find the answer in the dream I still have at least once a week — the one where Lila and I are black cats playing in a garden at night, running and leaping and pouncing with Nia in the moonlight.

DISCOVER MORE CHILLING STORIES FROM
MARY DOWNING HAHN

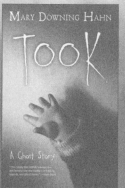